Alternative Truths III

ENDGAME

Also from B Cubed Press

Alternative Truths

More Alternative Truths: Tales From the Resistance

After the Orange: Ruin and Recovery

Alternative Theology

Digging Up My Bones,

by Gwyndyn T. Alexander

Firedancer,

by S.A. Bolich

Coming Soon

Alternative Apocalypses

Tales from the Space Force

Alternative Bedtime Reading for Progressive Parents

Alternative Truths III

ENDGAME

Edited by
Jess Faraday and Bob Brown

Cover Design
Sara Codair

Published by

B Cubed Press
Kiona, WA

Copyright© 2019 B Cubed Press
Interior Design (ebook) Bob Brown
Interior Design (print) Bob Brown
Cover Design Sara Codair
ISBN-13: 978-1-949476-05-7
Electronic ISBN-13: 978-1-949476-06-4
First Printing 2019
First Electronic Edition 2019

Copyright

Publisher's Introduction

This all started with a bottle of good rye whiskey and an election gone horribly wrong. A rough night to be an American.

As we inched towards the inauguration (with the largest crowds EVER) I watched with horror. My fingers found the keyboard in protest.

The writers in this, and the first two Alternative Truth volumes, were in the same place. Several of you suggested an anthology.

So we pushed back against the administration, not with bile and anger, but with the pen.

And readers loved it. They said yes, give us more. Here is more. More from the pens of some of the sharpest people I know.

It didn't happen alone.

I owe a debt of gratitude to Irene Radford, who guided me through the early days of B Cubed, Karen Anderson who kept me on an even keel as I looked for balance, Patrick Swenson for inspiring me, even when he didn't know it, and of course, Sue, a wife I don't deserve, who endures my endless dreams and notions, and lets me try.

Without Cheyenne Ockerman I'd just be making books that nobody ever saw (she manages promotions). Sara Codair, who worked into the night on the cover and Ben Howells who managed to proofread my editing.

And to the authors, the blessed, wonderful, and talented authors, who have so many options for their work and trusted B Cubed with it.

Thank you for the trust, the work, and the patience.

Bob Brown

Table of Contents

Foreword

Becky McFarland Kyle

"An end is only a beginning in disguise."
- *Craig D. Lounsbrough,*

America was birthed upon the radical notion "that all Men are created equal and are endowed by their Creator with certain unalienable Rights, that among these are Life, Liberty and the Pursuit of Happiness. That to secure these Rights, Governments are instituted among Men, deriving their just Powers from the Consent of the Governed."

While the obvious failures to immediately institute such high principles cannot be argued, in the 230 plus years since then, this land has seen many more new beginnings as the citizenship by war, ballot, or other measures, has no longer consented to discrimination and intolerance. Women have fought for and claimed the vote a century after the end of slavery, while Blacks challenged the notion that "separate but equal" facilities were not equal and demanded a place for their children in schools beside their white brothers and sisters.

Our nation has survived two world wars, countless conflicts, and terrorist attacks from both foreign and domestic nationals. Every ending has brought us strength and new challenges for the future.

These stories are written in the spirit that built this country, by sounding the call for restoration. To return to the promise of equality under the law, a strike against a would-be tyrant. This vision is of an America where future demagogues with a message of hate and intolerance will not be able to gain a hold, where social justice is not a pejorative, where people of different beliefs, origins, and abilities can work together to re-forge an America mended with hope and determination, and the oligarchs will no longer control a government in order to enrich themselves further. That among the unalienable rights we now add the right to medicine, living wages, clean water and air, and freedom to love who we will.

By reading these stories, you're opening yourself to the possibilities of new beginnings, both as suggested by the authors and from your own imaginings. This is the same kind of radical act that brought forth a nation, granted freedom to the oppressed, and helped fight and win wars against despots.

The creators of this volume will inspire you to begin yourself to take action to better this great country. As Margaret Mead said: "Never doubt that a small group of thoughtful, committed citizens can change the world; indeed, it is the only thing that ever has." Even a small act makes a difference: donate a book to veterans, register voters, write to your elected representatives and share your views and beliefs. None of these acts take a great deal of time or commitment, but are like tossing a rock into a pond. The effect will spread and encourage others to act for the betterment of our nation as well.

In the words of Barack Obama: "Change will not come if we wait for some other person, or if we wait for some other time. We are the ones we've been waiting for. We are the change that we seek."

Becky McFarland Kyle

Bathroom Breakdown

Jim Wright

President Trump has locked himself in the bathroom.

A press of concerned staffers gathers outside the door. Chief of Staff, Mick Mulvaney, pushes through the crowd and grasps the doorknob, giving it a firm jiggle.

Mulvaney: <sternly to the crowd> Quiet down. <to the door> MR. PRESIDENT!

Trump: <muffled sobs> GO AWAY!

Mulvaney: Mr. President, you've been in there long enough.

Trump: I SAID, GO AWAY!

Mulvaney: Mr. President, open this door immediately!

Crowd: <unintelligible>

Mulvaney: Oh right. Mr. President, pull up your pants FIRST. Then open this door!

 Crowd: <relieved sighs>

Trump: NO!

Mulvaney: No to the pants or no to the door?

Trump: I'M NOT CRYING!

Mulvaney: Nobody said you were, Mr. President. Except possibly on Twitter. And Facebook. And CNN. And...

Trump: I SAID GO AWAY! JUST GO AWAY! IT'S MY EXECUTIVE TIME!

Mulvaney: <angry> Dammit, put down that phone and open this door!

Trump: YOU CAN'T TALK TO ME LIKE THAT! I'M THE PRESIDENT! THE PRESIDENT! I DO WHAT I WANT!

Mulvaney:

Trump:

Crowd:

Mulvaney: <reasonable> Mr. PRESIDENT, hiding in the toilet doesn't keep Nancy Pelosi from being Speaker of the House.

Trump: <sound of vomiting and explosive diarrhea>

Mulvaney: <to the staff> Somebody get Ivanka up here. And call the plumbers.

The First Lady is Missing

Louise Marley

I feel worse about Nathan and Judy than I do about anyone else, even my son. They weren't the only ones responsible for this, of course, but they were always the closest agents to me. They'll be the ones to take the blame, Judy especially. I wish I could do something about that. I was their responsibility, and I know how much trouble they're going to be in. Judy has two young children. Nathan takes care of his elderly parents. They're sure to lose their jobs, if they haven't already. I worry about them all the time.

I'm aware that makes me look like a terrible mother. Uncaring. Selfish. But my son could hardly be safer than he is right now—especially now. Everyone will be on high alert.

But Nathan and Judy—I gave them the slip, and they weren't expecting it. I'm sorry, because they've been kind to me. Of course, they looked the other way when the President did the things he did, but they didn't have much choice. Ultimately, he's their boss, and he's a dangerous man to cross. No one knows that better than I do.

It's weird to watch the story grow on the television programs. They keep showing my picture from Inauguration Day, talking on and on and on, guessing, speculating, sometimes pretending they know what happened. It feels strange to be the object of all that chatter. Usually it's my husband they rattle on about, criticizing or praising or ridiculing.

I have to keep the sound off, but I watch the chyrons rolling beneath the faces of those familiar television reporters with their coiffed hair and glistening lips. When I first got here, the chyrons spoke to everyone's curiosity: *Where is she? Where's the First Lady?*

There were some imaginative ones: *Is the First Lady on a secret mission for the President?*

And there were critical ones: *The First Lady continues to shirk her duties.*

I knew that would come. The people who say such things don't know what it's like to have to hide your bruised face, or your broken finger, or the cut on your forehead where he threw the tv remote and, for once, hit his target. I can't go out to visit a hospital or speak to a ladies' luncheon when my eye is so swollen I can't put mascara on it, or when the outfit I was supposed to wear won't fit over the bandage on my knee from where he pushed me in the bathroom.

Nathan and Judy ran interference for me with my social secretary. They knew—probably the whole detail did—but what could they do? If they went to the head of the Secret Service, he'd have to speak to the President. Knowing my husband, he would probably fire the whole detail. No one outside the White House would believe them. No one would believe me. He would lie, and he's the President.

My husband is a very, very good liar. Maybe one of the best liars in the world. I figured that out, far too late. I don't think the rest of the country is ever going to understand just how adept he is at convincing people of untruths. It's a blessing, really, that he spends no time with our son. He would lie to him, too. He'd rather lie than not, to be honest. It comes naturally to him. It's his nature, repellent though it is. I wish I had understood that sooner.

But now I huddle, alone, in the elegant salon of my old friend's anchored yacht, *Sea Secret.* I watch the television news with no sound and all the blinds drawn tight, so no one will walk along the dock and suspect someone is in here.

Everything is battened down on the boat. The big galley is closed down, though the refrigerator is stocked so I have food. Everything on the decks is covered with tarps, and the crew has all been let go—for the duration, Tony said. I feel bad about them losing their jobs, but I was desperate, and I had literally one friend in the world I could trust.

At least, I hope I can trust him. My husband has a talent for making people betray the ones who trust them. As I said, he may be the best liar in the world.

As the days pass, the chyrons grow more and more intense. Most other news is being buried beneath the weight of the nation's—indeed, the world's—curiosity. The White House staff finally noticed my absence, my bed not slept in, my bathroom not used, the books and magazines in my sitting room undisturbed. People have started to ask questions.

The chyrons scream: *In a break with protocol, the First Lady is not at the President's side for a state dinner.* And *The First Lady cancels all appearances. Is she ill?* And, in an attempt to be jocular, *Call in if you've seen the First Lady!*

They would expect someone to recognize me if they saw me on the street, or in a car, or on a train. What they don't understand is how a designer dress, a designer hairdo, even a designer cosmetics job, can make a woman look utterly different from the way she looks every day. I don't look anything like that Inauguration Day image now. It's unlikely anyone would recognize me. No makeup. Sweatshirt, jeans, sneakers. My hair cut (badly, since I did it myself) so the gray roots show. I can see how I look in the stateroom mirror, a tired, too tall, too thin middle-aged woman.

And now, finally, the chyron I've been expecting. He will hate this one, because it means he can't ignore the situation any more. The press secretary will get questions. The secret service will show up in the Oval Office. The newspapers will go crazy. My parents will call, and insist on talking to him, and go to the television people when he refuses.

It's this one, the right one at last: *The First Lady is missing.*

And now that they've gotten there, the real questions start. *Was she kidnapped? Has she been poisoned, and is being kept in a secret hospital?* Or *Is the First Lady dead, and no one will admit it to the public?*

And, of course, *How could she escape the Secret Service? How could she get out of the White House with no one knowing?*

This is a good question. The White House is a fortress, despite its lovely old architecture and graceful interiors. The windows are impenetrable, the gardens are walled and guarded, every door is monitored. The Secret Service is an army, armed, dangerous, omnipresent. It's all designed to keep the President and staff safe, to keep dangers out.

And, as it turns out, to keep the First Lady in.

oOo

The 'how' of it all was worthy of a thriller. My friend—let's call him Tony—was a special friend of mine, of us both, really, from before the nightmare days, when a botched election landed me in a role I never wanted. I hadn't seen him for months, but Tony was a guest at one of the endless white-tie dinners we have to host at the White House. When I saw his name on the list, I managed to persuade one of the butlers—who are very sweet, and really do everything they can to make the First Lady happy—to switch the place tags, so Tony was seated beside me, on my left. On my right was an ambassador from some African country, whose language I don't speak and who speaks very little English. I was free to chat with Tony.

At first we talked about little things, his children, my son, their schools. We drank two glasses of wine apiece, and by dessert we were sharing more personal confidences. I was careful. I checked under my plate, and under the table, and felt around the bottom of my chair to be sure there were none of the listening devices my husband loves to plant. My friend's marriage was coming to an end, he said. Infidelity—hers, not his. I took his word for it.

My marriage was off limits for our conversation, but I did admit I hated D.C., I hated the job I had to do, and I especially hated living in the fishbowl of the White House. Tony knows my husband well, no doubt better than I do. He has known him for years. Did business with him, which means he got cheated by him. Tony had no illusions about what my marriage was like.

Months went by before I saw Tony again.

He was visiting with the President in the Oval, something about trade imbalances, which Tony is an expert in and which my husband misunderstands, as he misunderstands so many things. After the meeting, Tony asked one of the staff if he could say hello to me, his friend from the old days. The staff member escorted him to my office, and the two of us—with Nathan following at a discreet distance, sunshine glinting off his oversized sunglasses—went out to walk in the Rose Garden.

It was one of the first bits of luck I'd had in a long time. Nathan's second language is German. Tony speaks fluent French. Judy speaks French, too, but it wasn't her shift, so Tony and I could murmur to each other in French without worrying about being understood.

He said, "I have a crazy idea. You can laugh it off if you want."

"What is it?" *Qu'est-ce que c'est?*

"You can leave him. You *should* leave him."

"Leave him? As in, walk out?"

"Yes, walk out. Now. In the middle of his term. Say goodbye." *Au revoir.*

"He'd kill me."

"Only if he could find you. And I have an idea about that." He grinned down at me. He's tall enough to do that, and he looked good, clear skin, a full head of dark hair, naturally white teeth. I felt almost normal, walking with him, his hand under my arm, Nathan keeping a respectful distance because we were safe, there in the garden.

I said, "How, Tony? They watch me all the time!"

"Have you been down to the tunnels?"

We rounded the corner, into a shady spot where there was a bench to sit on. With a nod to Nathan, inviting him to join us if he liked, Tony and I sat down. Nathan stood a few steps away, his sunglasses flashing as he scanned the path and the lawn.

"Tunnels?" The word is the same in French, although pronounced differently from the English word. Tony's French is much better than mine, and I wasn't sure I had heard right.

"Yes. Beneath the house. There are dozens of them."

"There are?"

"There are. Sometimes you can see them on the tours."

"They don't let me take tours."

Tony kept his hands in his pockets, but his shoulder deliberately brushed against mine, and it felt good. I couldn't remember the last time someone touched me just because they wanted to. Even my son, with the cameras constantly flashing at us, won't hold my hand, or let me put my arm around his shoulders, or stand still for a hug.

"I'll get you a map," Tony said, his mouth so close to my ear I felt the warmth of his breath. Tony has sweet breath, smelling like citrus, or peppermint. My husband's is sour from all the junk he eats.

I thought the whole conversation was in jest, of course. Tony was fantasizing to make me feel better. I was sure it wasn't possible for me to really escape. And there was my son to think about. Of course, he's old enough now to make some decisions for himself, and he would certainly be safe...

I wouldn't have given Tony's wild suggestion another thought, except that night my husband knocked out one of my teeth and I had to be rushed—in secret—to a dentist to have it replaced. Judy went with me. I was so ashamed of the whole thing I couldn't meet her eyes. We didn't say a word, either on the way to the emergency dentist or on the ride back. I sensed her wish to reach out to me, possibly even touch my hand, but of course that wasn't in her job description. The other members of the detail kept their eyes averted from my swollen face. I don't know what Judy and Nathan told them, but none of them ever asked me a direct question, nor acknowledged my condition.

My husband is a violent man. His first wives both said so, but he said they were lying. I was younger then, more naive, and I believed him. He is a very, very good liar.

He is also a very unhappy man, a miserable man. In public, he shouts and preens and postures. In private, the frustrations of his life boil over. The constant fear of his inadequacy rises to the surface, and he lashes out. He breaks things—a vase, a glass, a chair. When I'm the closest thing, he breaks me.

Even full of pain medication, I couldn't sleep that night. I listened to the constant traffic noises, the comings and goings inside the White House, the drone of the television in my husband's bedroom.

I couldn't stop thinking about what awaited me in the coming days. They wanted me to give a speech, which terrified me. They wanted me to make a television appearance, which terrified me even more. They wanted me to fly overseas with the President on Air Force One, for the optics, they said. I wouldn't be able to get out of his sight for days on end.

My thoughts spun endlessly, and my eyes burned with sleeplessness.

In the small hours, I surrendered. In a bottom drawer I had hidden a little burner phone, a silly thing I had bought before moving here, impelled by some instinct, I suppose. I got out of bed, opened the drawer, and found the phone.

I texted one word to my old friend Tony: *Oui.*

oOo

Tony was right about the tunnels. There are so many of them! They lead to all kinds of places, meeting rooms and bunkers and bomb shelters. The entrances are disguised, and some of them are accessed through a door that looks like it opens onto a broom closet. There's a passage in the Oval Office, where you push on a panel and a wall opens, and you can descend into the tunnel system.

I did that. I told poor Judy I was going into the Oval to speak to my husband, and she didn't realize he had already gone to the residence. She should have known, of course, it was her job to know, but why should she doubt me? Me, who never has a word of her own to say, creeps around like a frightened kitten, cowers in corners and hides in her bedroom for hours on end. I'm sure they think of me as they might a pretty doll, one everyone likes dressing and playing with and taking pictures of, but one that gets put on a shelf at the end of the day. One that has no mind of her own, no will, no power.

So I went into the Oval, pressed the panel to open the door, closed it carefully behind me, and descended into the tunnels. I found the right one, with the help of the diagram Tony had mailed to me, tucked into a book. I walked for three hours, and emerged in a nondescript building designated for emergency evacuations. Tony was waiting for me, and drove me here, to his yacht.

That was seven days ago, and it seems we've been successful. No one but Tony knows where I am. When I cut off my hair, I wrapped it in a bag with rocks in it so it sank to the bottom of the Potomac. I found the jeans and sweatshirt and sneakers in one of the staterooms, along with some toiletries, which have come in handy. I watch the television because I don't have a computer or a smartphone, and I wouldn't dare log on to them even if I did. There are some battered paperbacks, and I read those. Mostly, I watch the silent news programs, and assess the building storm around my disappearance.

I slipped out once to go to the convenience store beside the moorage to buy juice and tea and newspapers, and no one noticed me. I felt triumphant about that. When I was safely closed into the salon again, I wondered if that was how it felt to be an ordinary woman—to go out and do something without anyone paying attention, to wander freely without having to explain, or dress for the cameras, or follow instructions.

The newspapers were cautious. *The New York Times* said almost nothing at first about my absence. *The Washington Post* let it go for three days before they reported a rumor that the First Lady was missing.

When I had been gone five days, *then* the chyrons on cable news began to get excited. The *Post* delved more deeply into the story, but of course, they don't have anything to go on. I'm not there. I'm gone. I'm missing, and no one knows why or how or if I'm coming back.

And the President? He hasn't said anything yet. Not a word.

He doesn't do press conferences, of course. He hates answering questions. He likes to call in to his favorite cable television channel, but he's careful which host to talk to, for the same reason. Even at Fox there are some actual journalists. He never does interviews unless he is promised in advance that they'll be friendly.

But now? He's trapped. He's going to have to say something, try to explain my absence. He'll try to feign worry, perhaps, though he's lousy at anything approaching empathy for another human being. What he's really feeling, I feel certain, is rage. Helpless fury. He's going to be humiliated, and I'm the cause.

Am I going back? Never.

Will he kill me if he knows where I am? Absolutely. I would not be the first.

Of course, he wouldn't do it with his own hands. But he has ways. He has people.

I make a cup of tea, and huddle on the low sofa in front of the yacht's big screen television. With the remote in hand, I click from one channel to the next. There are other stories in the news, of course, but I seem to be the predominant one. That is, my absence is the predominant one. I doubt very much anyone beyond my parents and one or two girlfriends actually care about me. I see shots from my wedding, pictures from when my son was small, a few posed fashion photos, but there's nothing personal. None of it is about me. It's all about the President's wife not being in her proper place.

It's the chyrons that tell the story, and they grow more and more frantic.

Secret Service desperately searching for the First Lady.

President mum on whereabouts of the First Lady.

FBI, CIA, and Interpol search for the First Lady of the United States.

First Lady sightings reported from a dozen countries.

Is the First Lady being held hostage?

Exclusive: First Lady being held in secret Russian gulag.

Did aliens steal the First Lady?

I couldn't have made my escape without Tony, of course, and I know that. Tony is a rich man, much richer in real terms than my husband is. Women like me, by which I mean women who look like me, tend to be surrounded by rich men, men who can buy who and what they want. My husband didn't buy me, exactly, but I was inexperienced enough to be dazzled by the gilded surroundings and the sparkling accessories of his life. I wasn't exactly in love with the man, but I was head-over-heels in love with the life I thought he was offering.

Now Tony is offering me a new life, and I want to take it. I'm not in love with him, either, but I like him very much, and I believe he likes me. That seems much more important to me now. And his wealth is essential to our plan. Wealth has always surrounded me, though it has never been my own wealth. It can be a cruel master.

So, the plan: I will wait here for another three weeks, until such an expensive boat being out of commission might command notice. Tony will hire a new crew, which I think will mean a captain, a cook, and a couple of other people, carefully selected and generously paid for their ability to be discreet. They're not to know who I am. The story will be that the yacht is being loaned to friends in France, and off we'll go. I won't have to worry about a passport or that sort of thing, because no one will know I'm here until we're in international waters. No one will know, again, that I'm here until we're safely docked in a tiny French port.

Obviously, this is a huge violation of my prenup. It also violates the postnup I signed after the dreadful results of the election, but I no longer care. Once he's out of office, and people aren't looking for me any longer, Tony promises to bring my son to my French hideaway. Until then, we'll let the mystery stand.

The Washington Post tells me my parents took my son home with them. My press secretary announced it was a planned vacation for him, but I know it was simply that my husband couldn't be bothered to deal with him. That was always my job, and it was the only job I cared about—until recently.

Fox News continues to claim that I'm on a secret mission for the President, and that he's keeping quiet about it until it's accomplished. MSNBC speculates that the First Lady committed suicide, but the President is too embarrassed to admit it. CNN takes the position that the First Lady has been kidnapped by some foreign agency, and that she'll be killed if anyone talks about it.

NBC, CBS, and ABC all limit themselves to counting the days since I was last seen in public.

It's a testament to how dangerous my husband is that neither my emergency dentist or any of the emergency physicians who treated my various injuries have spoken up. I don't blame them. They have careers and families to worry about. And though it's shockingly lonely, being completely isolated this way, I take comfort in knowing that I took control of my own life, for better or worse. I'm not that doll on the shelf anymore. I'm a graying middle-aged mother who still has half her life ahead of her and longs to spend it in freedom.

We planned carefully, Tony and I. It was hard, because we couldn't often even sit next to each other, much less be alone. Gifts and mail that come into the White House are closely vetted, but Tony and I share a love of reading, and he sent me books. They contained coded messages, disguised as dedications on the flyleaves: *Hope to see you in February. Hoping you and your family can join us on Sea Secret soon. Here's looking forward to that French holiday.*

I sent him books back, similarly inscribed. *February is perfect. We can't wait to see Sea Secret. Thank you for the map.*

I read the books he sent, too. He chose literary novels, mysteries, sometimes thrillers. My husband, who doesn't read at all, paid no attention to any of these exchanges.

We used the burner phone selectively, and only for the final details. When I left, I had it with me in my pocket. I threw it as far out into the river as I could, the moment I got out of Tony's car. I had another phone, of course, a better and more recent official one, but I left that in the residence. I double-checked all my old text messages on it, but there was nothing there either from or to Tony. In fact, there was little there at all. The tweets from me that people love to share are all written by staff, and they use their computers to do that.

Yet, despite all our care, I was afraid. When people trooped by on their way to another boat, or there were raucous parties on nearby yachts, I turned off the television so its light wouldn't penetrate the blinds. I hid in my stateroom in the darkness like an injured cat going to ground. It's a strange, distorted life, a reverse image of the one I had been living. No one sees me. No one speaks to me. I wear the same clothes every day, and I don't style what's left of my hair or put on makeup. I am invisible.

oOo

We thought, after a month had passed, that the story of the First Lady going missing would begin to die down. We were mistaken.

If the chyrons were anything to go by, the furor has only intensified. The four weeks are nearly up, but each week the story seems to get bigger. Wild stories are circulating, the President is under daily pressure to say something, and heads are rolling at the FBI and CIA and in the Secret Service. Even Congress is threatening to summon the President to speak to them about the First Lady's whereabouts. He has tweeted that it's none of their business, but it seems for once his tweets are having no effect.

I knew it would be bad. I didn't know it would precipitate a national crisis.

Now, and only now, are those who treated my injuries beginning to speak out. They start by telling reporters details off the record. Then, as their numbers grow, they gain confidence. Now the dentist, two emergency physicians, and my personal aesthetician, who has had to disguise my bruises many times, have been interviewed on television. My husband has plenty of enemies, and they're making the most of the scandal. It has become an international sensation.

Some are saying it could bring down the presidency, an outcome neither Tony nor I anticipated. I fear the whole thing has grown much too big for Tony to tolerate.

And now, as I stare at CNN in horror, I see that Tony has been called to the White House.

Everyone knows Tony's face, of course. Ostensibly, he is being called in as the President's old friend and confidante, to comfort a grieving husband whose wife has disappeared— or to provide cover if the husband has done something to his abused wife. But as I watch the silent pictures shown over and over on CNN and then the other cable channels, and finally on the mainstream news shows, it's clear that Tony has some sort of Secret Service escort—or FBI or whatever, I never can keep straight which department does which.

I turn off the television, and huddle on the couch in the salon, fearing the worst. Tony and my husband know a great deal about each other. They have had many business dealings over the decades. I'm afraid Tony is as vulnerable to blackmail as my husband is, and if my husband threatens him, he may have no choice but to give me up.

It occurs to me, too, for the first time, that Tony may have done all of this to hurt my husband rather than to help me. Their history is a complicated one. My husband is capable of any dirty trick he can think of. I wonder what he may have done to Tony. I wonder if I'll ever know.

Tomorrow is the day we're supposed to leave. The new crew will arrive. I will shut myself in the smallest stateroom, ready to fold myself up into a cargo compartment if necessary, until we know we're safe. At least, that was the plan. I have no way of knowing if it still is.

I don't sleep. I shower, and then stare at myself in the mirror. I don't even recognize my own face. I am pale, terribly thin, big-eyed and hollow-cheeked. Even my bust, once so important to my husband, looks shrunken. I look every single one of my years. He wouldn't have me now, I think. I am no longer a trophy wife. I'm a refugee.

I lock the stateroom door, as I'm supposed to. I lie on the bed, and watch the morning light begin to rise beyond the drawn blinds. Helpless in my ignorance of what's happening beyond my luxurious prison, I wait.

They arrive early, whoever they are. I hear someone in the galley. I hear several pairs of feet on the decks. I hear the rustle and bang and rush as the tarps are taken in and the blinds are lifted. My stateroom has no windows, only the single locked door, which I don't dare open. I cower on the bed, clutching a pillow to my middle.

Who is out there? I don't know. Is everything happening according to our plan? I don't know that, either.

The engine starts with a great thrumming vibration that I feel in my bones. There are calls back and forth, laughter, orders, shouts of farewell. The yacht begins to move, a gentle motion at first, as it glides out of its moorage, then a sense of gathering speed as it gets underway.

I lie back, and close my burning eyes. The rocking of the boat soothes my nerves, and a cold acceptance quiets my mind. Either I am making my escape, or I am not. Either I will be allowed to live the rest of my life in peace, or I will not.

Someone is guiding this boat to its destination, but it is not me. I have done what I can. I have earned my fate.

I sleep.

Waiting for Gustavo

DB Lipton

My sheet is yanked. I fall from the top bunk, cracking my head on the cement floor.

"Wake up, Yarborough." Hunzeker is already in uniform, an AK over his shoulder, heavy bandoliers criss-crossing his chest. "Move! Enemy's at the gates!" I dress while Hunzeker glares, sweat streaking his gaunt face. He looks hungrier every day.

In the barracks doorway, Hunzeker grips my shoulders, yells, "Who's coming today?"

Despondent, I answer, "Gustavo." There was a time when I tried to match his enthusiasm, but the energy is hard to summon when my stomach is eating itself. Seeing my dispassion, Hunzeker's gray eyes go wide. He head-butts my nose, barks, "Look alive!" and dashes out the door. I remind myself that I really need this job.

Outside, heat flashes across my scalp as I survey our post. In the middle of the Chihuahuan Desert, Border Crossing Checkpoint A527 is a twelve-foot square gated passageway cut out of the 1200 mile Victory Wall of United Heroes to which we have pledged our lives. Hunzeker and I swore an oath to defend our portion of the thirty-foot tall stack of precast concrete and steel rebar, stretching east and west beyond the horizon.

Hunzeker applied for the position because he believed his country was in danger of infiltration by bloodthirsty criminals. I just needed a steady job. The United States shuttered more than half its public education program to pay for this behemoth, putting teachers like me out of work. I used to tell my students that a person cannot be "illegal". Now I'm expected to shoot anyone trying to cross under, over, or through our beloved wall.

Fortunately, nothing happens. Nobody comes, nobody goes. But it's lonely, especially since the radio died. And then there's the hunger.

oOo

At first, trucks rumbled by every few weeks, dropping off crates of supplies. Over time, deliveries thinned. First I noticed less fresh fruit. Word was that without migrant pickers, those crops were too expensive, save for the very rich. "Fuck fruit," Hunzeker said, but I missed the large red apples, hard as wood. When I mourned this loss aloud, Hunzeker looked at me like I'd just asked for naked pictures of his sister. "Get your mind right, Yarborough."

Now resources are so scarce that even the Cheetos and Gatorade we're expecting will be a feast. The last crate included a form letter commending our continued sacrifice while the food budget shifted to labor and building materials. Canada was gouging us on sand and gravel while labor was hard to find. After the first hundred miles of the wall, built by loyal but unskilled volunteers, crumbled under the weight of too many gargoyles, the government concluded it should be constructed by experienced craftsmen and engineers. But those who were willing were also expensive. Consciences could be bought, but not cheaply.

After closing schools, they siphoned funds from Medicare. Hunzeker mentioned his mother lost a leg when she couldn't afford her diabetes medication. Before I could ask about it, he pulled his gun and fired south toward the wall until the clip was empty. Ammunition has been eerily plentiful.

oOo

By midday, we've finished the last of our sour coffee. It is 110 degrees in the sparse shade of our lone mesquite tree. Hunzeker says sunblock is for Frenchmen, so his face is red as boiled lobster. On the wall, beneath the words "Days Without Enemy Invasion," Hunzeker uses a power drill to grind a tally mark beside countless others. It isn't an accomplishment. We've never repelled or apprehended anyone. I've wanted to ask Hunzeker if he thought other posts see any action, but it's never been worth agitating him. He steps back, smiling like a golden retriever, and announces, "Gustavo's coming today."

Gustavo is due any day now with resupplies of food rations, and maybe soap, booze, and porn. It's a fantasy we've tacitly agreed to embellish, though when I suggested Gustavo might bring some books, Hunzeker boxed my ear.

"How do you know he'll come today?" I ask.

"He has to. We're out of food."

I admit, I've enjoyed succumbing to Hunzeker's party pride, his unwavering faith that we're valued by those in power because of what we do in their name. But today my hunger speaks louder than his zealotry. Ignoring Hunzeker's gun, I blurt, "Maybe a thirty billion dollar wall wasn't a good idea."

He turns to me, eyes narrow. "This wall is my life. It is our nation's will."

"Our nation's will left me unemployed," I say.

"You were a schoolteacher. Glorified daycare. They did you a favor. Now you have purpose."

"Who do you think is coming here? What are we guarding? There are no schools, no jobs and no one who matters gives a shit. If you do manage to find work, you'll probably get shot. And if you somehow survive that, you'll die anyway when you can't afford a surgeon to remove the bullet."

Hunzeker is in my face now, shouting, "If you hate this country so much, get the fuck out." Squinting against blazing sunlight, I scan the wall, wondering if one actually did try to get over it, could they? When I turn back, Hunzeker's hands are around my throat.

Just then we hear buzzing, faint at first, then distinct. A small vehicle being pushed to its limit. A motorcycle bursts into view. The rider whips his helmeted head, startles, and wipes out in the dirt embankment. He rolls several times, takes a moment, then stands unhurt, removing his helmet. Dark hair falls to his shoulders.

"Border Guard?" We nod. He says, "There is no Border Guard. Victory Wall of United Heroes employees are relieved from duty. Thank you for your service."

"But," Hunzeker stutters, "I swore an oath."

The rider shrugs. "The wall is finished. Now go home before you starve." He replaces his helmet and speeds away. Hunzeker and I stand in his dust, watching him go.

"Do you think that was Gustavo?" I ask.

"No," says Hunzeker. "Gustavo will come tomorrow."

Tyrannus ab ultima Epistulae

Frédéric J.A.M. Poirier

In the halls of the Museum of Memory there is a plaque.
It tells of time before.
Before the world media collectively went silent.
Before the internet was broken, and frozen in time on buried servers.
It has a small bird engraved in the upper right hand corner.
The date is a date we all know.

The plaque reveals the abject emptiness that caused that date to be irrevocably etched in our collective memory.
The title on the plaque is simple: "The Last Tweets"

Donald J. Trump @*realDonaldTrump*
@ all the losers and very bad people who threaten us.
We've got the best smartest stablest nukes. You're all
FIRED !!

Donald J. Trump @*realDonaldTrump*
My generals are corrupt liberal snowflakes. They won't
fire the nukes. Fine! I'm calling all the world leaders, and
letting them know we're going to war. I will run in
unarmed if I have to.

Donald J. Trump @*realDonaldTrump*
North Korea and Russia have great strong leaders.
They're not afraid to send nukes, unlike my snowflake
generals. Nukes are coming! What are we gonna do,
generals? Are you going to do what you're paid to do, or
should I fire you too?

The Ballad of Cadet Bone Spurs

Larry Hodges

(Sung to the tune of "*The Ballad of Jed Clampett*," with apologies to Lester Flatt and Earl Scruggs)

Come and listen to my story 'bout a prez named Trump,
A bad president, turned the country to a dump,
And then one day he was screaming lies and bile,
And up from the congress comes an Impeachment Trial.

Justice that is.
Truth told.
American glee.

Well the first thing you know ol' Trump's a prisonaire,
Mueller proved a Russian love affair,
Congress voted, "Prison is the place you oughta be,"
So the FBI arrested Trump and Leavenworth he be!

Locked up, that is.
No parole.
Prison bars.

Well now it's time to say goodbye to Bones Spurs and his kin,
They're bitter lifers now and hate your guts for droppin' in.
You're all invited now to Make it Great Again,
A task made much more easy with a prez who's got a brain.

No more lies, that is.
Faux News quelled.
No government standoff.

Y'all never vote stupid again, y'hear?

Politics As Usual

K.G. Anderson

"We can't let evil change our life and change our schedule."
— *U.S. President Donald Trump, October 27, 2018,* in
the wake of the Pittsburgh synagogue killings.

There was no way to trace the communications. The code words had been set up months ago and distributed online through closed groups.

Now, someone was broadcasting the code words through public channels—and the terrorists went into action.

It began with a massacre at an urban synagogue in late October—the first in a 10-day series of massacres that preceded the 2020 elections.

Each shooting and bombing took place in a blue city, where voters traditionally supported progressive candidates. No shootings took place in the red suburbs.

Each shooting was perpetrated by a man quickly described as a "lone shooter with a history of mental illness."

Each of the shooters drove vans covered in the same political stickers and each wore the same uniform: A motley assembly of second-hand military and security gear, with a bulletproof vest.

Every shooter was captured alive. Despite being heavily armed, they offered little or only token resistance to the police. One reporter's smartphone captured a shooter addressing the officer who led him from the scene as "Brother." The officer grimaced.

Public defenders represented the shooters at their bail hearings. But David Means, a journalist for several liberal news blogs, discovered that the papers subsequently filed with the courts were all signed by criminal defense attorneys from a major national law firm.

"Where are these 'lone shooters' getting the money to hire these lawyers?" Means asked on one of his obscure blogs. "Or, why is this particular firm offering legal defense services for free?" Larger papers failed to pick up this story, scrambling as they were to prepare in case the next shootings took place in one of their own cities.

The president urged calm, vowing America would not be cowed.

A nervous Election Day began with a mass killing in a college town in Connecticut. Fifty-three students, professors, and university employees were mowed down as they waited in line to vote outside the college's divinity school. Soon the internet was flooded with pictures of young students on their knees beside fallen friends on the leaf-strewn sidewalk, in stark silhouette against classic white New England buildings.

"Terror at the Polls," the online headlines blared.

Within minutes, tens of thousands of people nationwide went online to demand that the elections be halted.

"We fear for our lives if we try to vote!" one woman wrote.

"I've risked my life for my country in the field," a veteran posted. "Now I have to do it while voting."

Fox News downplayed the events. Sean Hannity told his listeners that right-thinking Americans had nothing to fear.

Rush Limbaugh laughed at the idea of being afraid to vote. "Just take your guns to the polls," he said. "Oh wait, you don't have any."

Democratic leaders, citing the string of attacks on blue cities, charged voter suppression.

"Unfortunately, closing the polls is a state and local decision, outside our purview," a spokesperson for the Federal Elections Commission said. Three of the commissioners decried the situation as "voter intimidation." But the other three dismissed the Connecticut college killings as "an isolated incident," pointing out that the 10 preceding mass killings had not taken place at a polling place and had nothing to do with the elections.

Rumors raced through the internet. There were rumors that polling places in Atlanta, Austin, Dallas, Nashville, Boston, and Miami and other major cities would be targeted in the next hours. Tens of thousands of people in those cities posted that they were cancelling plans to vote for fear of being shot.

Meanwhile, tens of thousands of people in red precincts posted pictures of themselves exiting their polling places, wearing stickers that read, "I'M not AFRAID to VOTE."

A reporter asked two voters exiting the polls in his own suburban town where the stickers came from. "I don't know—I guess they just had them at the polls, somewhere," one answered.

Election officials throughout the country were wringing their hands. No one was prepared to take the responsibility for closing polling places on Election Day. Republican officials issued statements insisting that "Americans will not be intimidated by an isolated incident in a tiny college town." Democratic officials urged people to "Stay alert," and promised police presence at polling stations.

There was a collective sigh of relief when the polls closed at 8 p.m. on the West Coast.

"Not a single ADDITIONAL mass shooting has occurred," Means tweeted. "And sadly, in this country, that constitutes 'good' news."

In urban areas, voter turnout was down 30 to 50 percent from 2016 levels. In suburban and rural areas, it was down 3 percent. Nearly every progressive challenger to a Republican incumbent was solidly defeated. (The only exceptions were in Oregon, where mail-in voting had taken place weeks earlier, and two Democrats defeated Republicans to take House seats.) The president won re-election and claimed the Electoral College by a landslide.

"We are not afraid! We are not afraid! We did not let the actions of one single lone person, one guy who acted completely alone, with a clear history of not being mentally in good shape, get in the way of us voting for, voting for and electing, the very best candidates, real winners, in our great country," the president said in a speech to the National Rifle Association the following morning. The NRA speech had been scheduled, his staff said, months in advance and they wanted to stick to the president's schedule.

"It's business as usual," the White House spokesperson told reporters. "We will not be intimidated."

The White House issued no official statement that night when a bomb went off in the basement of an inner-city church in Baltimore that had been used as a polling place the previous day. The explosion destroyed the building, injuring an employee who'd been cleaning the pastor's office.

"Some people just can't keep on schedule," the president tweeted that night. The tweet quickly vanished.

Act Three

David Gerrold

Here is a theory—a speculation.

Trump's continuing weird behavior, his inability to function as an adult, might be explainable with a single sentence: "Grampa is sundowning."

What is equally likely is that the reality of the midterms is finally sinking in. The Republicans have lost the House of Representatives and one source suggests as many as 85 separate investigations into Trump's "badministration" are not only possible, but inevitable. Myself, I'd put the number closer to 12—the seriously damaging ones. 85 is overkill, it would keep the house from doing anything else.

The Republicans, especially Trump, are looking at a horrifying political reality—being held accountable.

There are no good options for the party and the 2020 elections are already stacked against keeping control of the senate, regardless of who wins the presidency. Something like 23 Republican seats are up for reelection. The blue wave and the pink wave and the brown wave and the Parkland wave—all those will not be a one-time event. The various waves are even more energized now.

So what's going on in the badministration? I suspect that various scenarios and game plans are being discussed—I suspect that Trump is not part of those conversations. The man has nothing substantial to contribute.

His deterioration may have become so severe that he is no longer even pretending to do the job. But what scenarios? What game plans?

Hard to say. Based on the evidence, the Republican party is as much divorced from reality as Trump. The obstructionist wing of the Republican party is not going to give up their long-held beliefs that all Democrats have horns and tails and listen to Metallica records played backward.

Perhaps a few Republicans have finally figured out that they have gotten as much out of Trump as they can. They got their tax breaks and they got their hands on public lands and they got all the judges they can get. But Trump's increasingly bizarre behavior has become a national and international liability. Whatever advantage there might be to keeping him, there is greater advantage for the party in discarding him now before he does even greater damage to their 2020 chances. There might be a chance for the Republicans to save something out of this mess if they cut certain losses now.

The above analysis is viable only if there are any Republicans who are still in touch with the realities of the situation, and based on the evidence, the above is more in the realm of wishful thinking than probability.

So... something might be up. Or maybe not. Maybe no one has any idea what to say right now. Maybe they've noticed that certain words and deeds have created a backlash severe enough to be noticeable.

But the most likely possibility—and this is also a speculation—is that various lawyers have been quietly informed about various impending subpoenas and indictments. They may have been presented with situational ultimatums. I suspect that a lot of people are waiting for hammers to fall, shoes to drop, things to be revealed. That's when the real scramble begins.

Chaos theory (crudely explained) suggests that when a curve reaches a point where further acceleration is impossible, it breaks. That instance is called "a catastrophe." At that point, there is no predictability because the curve is no longer a predictor. The 1929 stock market crash is a textbook example.

It is possible that we have reached that point in American politics—where Donald Trump and the fascist wing of the Republican party have pushed the American government to the limits of where it can go without breaking. It is possible that the badministration has reached its own inevitable catastrophe point.

The one thing that is clear to me, and has been clear for a long time, is that there is a faction in the Republican party that does not consider consequences—a belief system so divorced from reality that self-awareness is impossible. The result is a behavior that defies common sense. Had there been any common sense in the party, they would have found a way to stop Trump before he even got in reach of the nomination. Had there been any common sense, they'd have sabotaged his election campaign. Had there been any common sense, they'd have learned something from the failures of the Bush administration. The Republican party abandoned common sense when they embraced the racists and the religious fanatics—so hungry for power that they adopted the tactics of Richard Nixon instead of the policies and strengths of Dwight D. Eisenhower.

Just as the Democrats have had to periodically reinvent themselves to remain relevant, it may be that it is long past time for the Republicans to reinvent themselves. But don't hold your breath. The people who hijacked the Republican party as an access to power are not going to give up their hold on the party, nor will they willingly give up their hold on our government.

If I were bold enough to predict anything, I would say it's time to fasten our seatbelts, it's going to be a bumpy ride.

Alternative Truths III: ENDGAME

Stupid?

Adam-Troy Castro

Another anguished post from a Trump supporter: "Why do liberals think Trump supporters are stupid?"

The serious answer.

Sigh; we do sometimes fall into that rhetorical trap, out of frustration, but if we were to be 100% honest with you we would admit that we find quite a few people on our own side stupid as well, mostly people who have boiled all the complicated issues into slogans and really don't comprehend what they're saying. I think you guys probably look at the dumber of your compatriots and think, "Jesus, this guy's barely rubbing his brain cells together, but at least he can wave a sign."

No, this is what we really think about Trump supporters, the rich, the poor, the malignant and the innocently well-meaning, the ones who think and the ones who don't.

That when you saw a man who had owned a fraudulent University, intent on scamming poor people, you thought "Fine."

That when you saw a man who had made it his business practice to stiff his creditors, you said, "Okay."

That when you heard him proudly brag about his own history of sexual abuse, you said, "No problem."

That when he made up stories about seeing Muslim-Americans in the thousands cheering the destruction of the World Trade Center, you said, "Not an issue."

That when you saw him brag that he could shoot a man on Fifth Avenue and you wouldn't care, you chirped, "He sure knows me."

That when you heard him illustrate his own character by telling that cute story about the elderly guest bleeding on the floor at his country club, the story about how he turned his back and how it was all an imposition on him, you said, "That's cool!"

That when you saw him mock the disabled, you thought it was the funniest thing you ever saw.

That when you heard him brag that he doesn't read books, you said, "Well, who has time?"

That when the Central Park Five were compensated as innocent men convicted of a crime they didn't commit, and he angrily said that they should still be in prison, you said, "That makes sense."

That when you heard him tell his supporters to beat up protesters and that he would hire attorneys, you thought, "Yes!"

That when you heard him tell one rally to confiscate a man's coat before throwing him out into the freezing cold, you said, "What a great guy!"

That you have watched the parade of neo-Nazis and white supremacists with whom he curries favor, while refusing to condemn outright Nazis, and you have said, "Thumbs up!"

That you hear him unable to talk to foreign dignitaries without insulting their countries and demanding that they praise his electoral win, you said, "That's the way I want my President to be."

That you have watched him remove expertise from all layers of government in favor of people who make money off of eliminating protections in the industries they're supposed to be regulating and you have said, "What a genius!"

That you have heard him continue to profit from his businesses, in part by leveraging his position as President, to the point of overcharging the Secret Service for space in the properties he owns, and you have said, "That's smart!"

That you have heard him say that it was difficult to help Puerto Rico because it was the middle of water and you have said, "That makes sense."

That you have seen him start fights with every country from Canada to New Zealand while praising Russia and quote, "falling in love" with the dictator of North Korea, and you have said, "That's statesmanship!"

That you have witnessed all the thousand and one other manifestations of corruption and low moral character and outright animalistic rudeness and contempt for you, the working American voter, and you still show up grinning and wearing your MAGA hats and threatening to beat up anybody who says otherwise.

What you don't get, Trump supporters in 2018, is that succumbing to frustration and thinking of you as stupid may be wrong and unhelpful, but it's also...hear me...charitable.

Because if you're NOT stupid, we must turn to other explanations, and most of them are *less* flattering.

Alternative Truths III: ENDGAME

Fortunate Son

Paula Hammond

"It was the smell that stuck with you. Burnt earth. Metallic Sulphur. An acrid tang of gunpowder and machine oil that clogged your nose and made every meal taste like over-broiled meat. On top of that lay the stink of men and jungle. Some days, it was impossible to tell where one began and the other ended. Everything was damp, clotted with mud and the funk of decay. After a couple of weeks, your clothes became slick with black grease, encrusted with salt. No matter how wet you got, it would never wash out.

"The thing that surprised me most, though, was the cold. I didn't expect the jungle to be cold, but it was. The monsoon rains could drench you in seconds and leave you shivering. I was never dry. Not once in seven months. That might seem like a small thing but in-country, on patrol, your days shrink down to a world of small things. That stench that never leaves you, that itch you can never scratch, wet feet, c-rations—pallid meat in a pool of congealed fat—always eaten cold because there's never enough heat tabs to go round. And leeches. They got everywhere. I have a reputation for being prissy—uptight even—but you wouldn't say that if you'd seen me drop my pants and ask my buddy to check my ass for leeches. Trust me, that's one place you *do not* want bug spray."

Donnie paused the video with a smile. He could see, captured in that grainy footage, the small group of veterans whooping appreciatively behind him. He remembered that he'd promised his campaign manager he wouldn't tell 'the ass gag' but—hell—it never hurt to make a joke at your own expense. Odd how, almost 20 years later, he'd been able to laugh about it. Men had lost their minds over less. First weeks out, he thought he would.

Back then, he was just the FNG—the Fucking New Guy—the butt of everyone's joke.

"Shit, don't you know this boy's a mill-eon-air?" That was Jonas, a soft-spoken New Englander with a bum-fluff beard. The squad comedian, he would spell the word out just like that, grinning like it was the most ridiculous thing he'd ever heard in his whole life.

"No shit? That true?" The wide-eyed kid from Kansas would say. George was on his second tour, still flinched at gun-fire, still said Grace, still brushed his teeth every night, and was still genuinely surprised at pretty much everything.

"Yeah, Donnie's father could buy this whole damn country iffenn he wanted to, ain't that right?" Clay chipped in. Clay—no one knew if that was his first or last name—liked to play the dumb old Southern boy but Donnie knew Clay'd been headed for medical school before the draft. If he'd been rich and white he'd never have even been called up.

"Damn. Couldn't you buy yourself out of this shit-hole? Get yourself a nice desk job?" Perrie's nervous crescendo and habitual knuckle-cracking betrayed the fact that he'd been the FNG just a month ago.

"Donnie's a pat-ri-ot, ain't that right?" That was Carlos. Hendrix wanna-be. Foul-mouthed card-sharp. Mexican by birth, snarling Texan by inclination.

"Id-i-ot more like," Jonas chipped in.

"I heard that." The twin echo was the Sams. No one could figure the Sams. They seemed to be joined at the hip, but as they were the meanest bastards this side of the line, no one asked and no one told.

Donnie always took it in good humor. They'd been having the same conversation every night for the past three weeks. He knew the routine.

Now it was Sarge's turn. "Cut it out boys, the kid's alright." The big man hailed from some mid-West town no one could remember the name of, and looked like every generic Sarge from every war film you'd ever seen. Spoke like it too. That same mix of fatherly despot that had steadied the hearts of boys on battlefields ever since the Revolutionary War. Clay often claimed they made Sarges by the gross and shipped one out with every squad.

When he'd first arrived, they'd ridden him pretty hard. Especially when they learned he'd dodged the draft, not once, but three times. No one blamed him. None of them really wanted to be there, but there was something about that sort of privilege that rankled. The fact that he'd volunteered rather than take a fourth deferment kept the jokes the right side of friendly. He still had no idea why he'd done it, but he suspected it was sheer arrogance.

He'd been packed off to a military academy as a wild teen. Emerged, five years later, thinking he knew more about combat and weaponry than most anybody. He'd always been competitive, always wanted to lead. Been polished and prepared for it. Part of him wanted to prove himself, to go in as a humble grunt and come back as an officer and a hero. It hadn't taken him long to realize that war wasn't about trials and triumphs. It was days of boredom and discomfort punctuated by flashes of fear. After a month, the height of his ambition was a dry pair of socks and a bug-free bivouac.

School had taught him how to give orders but, he reflected, it had taken 'Nam before he'd learnt how to take them. It had chipped him away and revealed someone new. The final residue of that haughty kid who believed some people were born special was washed away the day a short-order cook from Baltimore saved his life. If he was honest, he liked that new guy a lot better than the old one.

Usually, when he told his Purple Heart story, he shrugged it off: "Got careless. Caught a bullet. Thank God for small mercies."

He rarely told it as it was, and when he did, it never went down well. One time, as guest speaker at his old military academy, he'd spoken for less than five minutes. In that time, he'd watched a sea of rich, confident faces balk and turn pale.

"I don't even remember getting hit," he began. "One minute I was listening to the sound of boots sucking their way out of the mud, the next, it was like I'd been punched with a cattle prod. Took me a while to realize I was the one doing the screaming. Forget what you've heard. There's no pain like it. It owns you. No way are you going to get up and carry on fighting. Oh, you'll try, because that's how you've been trained, but all I could do was flap around, howling and twisting as though somehow I could shake myself free of the torment. Then suddenly, it got hot. Volcanic. I could feel the heat spread down my body, like someone had dipped me head-first in boiling water. The world collapsed. Darkness swallowed me and, when I came round, there was Sam Two, leaning over me.

Now, this son-of-a-bitch was a natural-born solider. He'd been the one to call out my sorry FNG-ass for every fuckup since I'd landed in the jungle, and here he was asking me about family. Had I got anyone special? And, somehow, that was more terrifying than anything I'd experienced up to that point. I knew, then, I was in serious trouble. No one is ever ready to die but I was twenty-three years old. No age at all. So, yes, I howled, and I raged, and I called out to every deity I could think of. Then the morphine hit and things got weird.

My brain was floating in a euphoric sea. I'd forgotten why I was lying in the sludge. Kept trying to get up. And there was Sam Two, with his hands pressed on my chest. I twisted my head and looked down and, as I watched, I saw blood—my blood—oozing through his outstretched fingers. The pain's gone and so's the fear. I'm a bystander rubbernecking at my own death and this bastard's in my face, talking about his life, his hopes, the world he wants. I want him to shut the hell up, but he keeps at it. Anything to keep me focused. I ended up hating and loving this guy because he wouldn't let me sleep. Because that's what you want to do. Go to sleep. Only if that happens, it's the last thing you'll ever do."

They hadn't invited him back.

That was a long, long time ago now, but in many ways he owed everything to the war. To those guys. One of the first things he'd done when he returned from 'Nam was to set up a fund management company to help veteran start-ups. His father had refused to help—he really didn't like Donnie's new friends—but the Trump name still bought a lot of credit. Soon he had fingers in some very lucrative pies. Not only were his investments sound but, when he entered politics, those businesses threw themselves behind him too.

Looking at the video now, he recognized many of those faces in the crowd, but the war had whittled away so many.

Sarge had died first, drowning in his own blood when an SKS ripped his chest to confetti. Carlos stepped on an anti-personnel mine, cut off mid-sentence, as his body somersaulted through the air. Sam One had fallen in a pit trap and took a punji stick to the groin. Sam Two hanged himself in his parents' garage, one year-to-the day later. They never knew why.

He had known those men more completely than he knew his own family but, in battle, death blindsides you. Whenever he thought about those he'd lost, he remembered them in staccato. No goodbyes, no time for grief. Just stark moments followed by a cocktail of adrenaline, shock, euphoria, and guilt. You dealt and moved on. Today, though, as he watched the documentary celebrating his 90th birthday, his mind kept drifting to the past.

The same thing had happened all those years ago as he stood on the podium preparing to become America's 42nd President. He pressed play, and re-lived the moment. He saw his younger self shudder. Then silence. A few echoing coughs. His campaign manager starting to move forwards. Some speculative comments from the reporter. More silence.

Later, he'd blamed nerves but the truth was the ghosts simply wouldn't lie still.

There he'd been, in the glare of the world's press, and all the well-designed fancy sound-bites vanished. All he could think of was those painful, pointless deaths. And his words—so carefully prepared—suddenly seemed painful and pointless too. So, he had put down his notes, taken the breaks off his wheelchair, and slowly maneuvered himself around the oversized lectern. Then, he'd taken a deep breath, and given the speech that would define his Presidency.

"58,148 Americans were killed in Vietnam" he said. "75,000 were left disabled. Of those killed, 61 percent were younger than 21-years-old. 2.7 million served. Two-thirds of those were volunteers. Ask any solider and they will tell you that there's no such thing as a good war but 'Nam gave me two things: friends and a purpose. I wanted to make sure that no American would ever have to die in a foreign land again. I wanted to put America First. To take back control for the people. It's been a long, long road and I want to thank all those who have walked it with me, especially Bill, who believed enough to join me on this momentous journey."

Donnie remembered how untiringly Clinton had campaigned for the Democratic nomination and it had been a real blow when he'd lost. It had taken all of his charm to persuade him to come on board as his running mate. Although he hadn't served, many of their generation shared Bill's opposition to the war, and Donnie felt that added balance to their campaign. Besides, he genuinely liked the Clintons. Hilary was an incredible woman. The sort of woman he'd have wanted by his side, if a bullet lodged in his spine hadn't set his life on another path.

The press had called it The Dream Team. Clinton: the charming joker, the family man, with practical experience in government. Trump: a touch of steel, a successful business man, a veteran who was considered a safe pair of hands. They'd championed workers' pay, women's issues, civil rights. Donnie firmly believed in gay marriage—a controversial policy—but he always said that equality was an all-or-nothing deal. The easier sells had been universal health, green energy. The liberals loved them, the blue collars loved them, the environmentalists loved them. Their only real opposition had been the gun lobby who'd tried to paint them as unpatriotic for their pledge to repeal the Second. As a draft dodger Bill had taken a lot of flack on that front but, in the end, it didn't matter. They'd carried 32 states to Bush's 18.

Donnie sighed, pressed pause once more, and looked at the crowd frozen in that moment of celebration. People talked about his presidency as a turning point. Two terms that had changed everything. But he knew that, at the end of the day, it had little to do with him. He was just the catalyst. He'd known, then, that people were ready for change. Known that together they'd Make America Great Again.

Final Tweet

Nathan Ockerman

Some people have no consideration. Here, the President of the United States sits in his elegant, but admittedly sub-par, bedroom enjoying his morning Diet Coke, catching up on today's news and some asshole is pounding on his door. There was shit he would have to deal with later—a pointless mountain of papers sitting at his office desk, fires caused by his worthless, backstabbing, opportunistic "support" team, the phone calls he would then have to make to help people see things his way, all while a country of naive idiots drank up the lies fed to them by Fake News that he would have to set straight. It was more than any one person should be expected to handle. So, as he was entitled to, he took a few minutes between eight and eleven every morning to relax and prepare himself for the onslaught with some soda and TV. But now, he wasn't even allowed to do that, because *someone* was *pounding* on his door.

"Whoever you are, shut up and go away. This is like, very possibly, probably, my only time I have to myself all week. Goodbye."

"But Mister President, I need—"

The President turned up the volume on his TV and chuckled as the voice behind the door was drowned out by a fast-food double bacon cheeseburger commercial. He made a mental note to have Mike Pence get him two or three for his lunch. He'd fire the idiot door minion later—you had to do that to incompetent staff, especially ones who couldn't understand personal space.

Unbelievable, he thought, downing the last of his cola.

The commercial ended, and the television blared out the comforting Fox News jingle, spinning block letters of patriotic colors dancing in time with the music until they faded away, leaving three smiling anchors on a plush leather couch.

"Welcome back," the woman said, as the other two angled toward the audience. "Before the break we were discussing the proposed legislation that would make it easier for tens of thousands of illegal aliens to suddenly become voting citizens... they call them Dreamers, I call then invaders. If they want to live in our country, they should come here right the first time."

The President couldn't help but smile. With all the Fake News out there he was proud to only pay attention to truthful journalists. He pulled his phone from his robe pocket—his favorite application was already open, waiting for his thoughts.

Donald J. Trump @realDonaldTrump
@FOXNEWS
Good call on Horible Dem bill. These "kids" are just here to take welfair. NO ones asking why they're allowed to cross the border in first place. Dumb. We need the #WALL.

He added the tweet to the impressive list of his insights over the years. Heck, when this President stuff was done, he could transfer the list into a book, call it "Presidential Wisdom", or "Notions of Leadership", something catchy that would bring in a good chunk of money. He could have interns pull it together, wouldn't even need to pay them, they could put it on their resume. He should charge them for the privilege.

The President slipped the phone back in his pocket and grabbed another Diet Coke from the mini-fridge. He had popped the can's tab when there was another knock at the door. More insistent this time.

"Go away!"

"Mr. President we need to speak with you. It's urgent."

"Whatever it is, it can wait. I'm busy at the moment."

The locked door handle jiggled as the new voice said, "Mr. President there's been—"

"Fuck. Off!" He shouted and threw the can at the door. It bounced off the cheap molding and sprayed light brown foam as it spun to a stop on the carpet. Footsteps retreated down the hallway—at least this one was smart enough to take a hint. The President looked at the mess dripping down the wall, already drying sticky in some places. Nothing he had to worry about. He was pissed at whoever-that-was for making him waste a new coke; whatever, he'd fire that guy too. Unbelievable.

Back to the mini-fridge, cursing the fact that he couldn't get five minutes to himself. He, the most powerful man in the free world, who could bring down empires and fix economies on a whim, apparently wasn't even allowed to watch the morning news. Where was the loyalty? The respect for what *he* needed? He cracked the can and took a long drink, relishing the bubbly burn of carbonation cleaning the walls of his throat as it went down. *No better way to wake up*, he thought.

"Next up we have some breaking news about President Donald Trump. Early this morning, a number of documents, internal memos, and transcripts, reportedly from the Trump campaign, the offices of the president's legal defense team, and financial records of former Speaker of the House were emailed to Mueller's office, the FBI, Homeland Security, and the Pentagon." He paused for a full ten seconds. "It also appears they were also posted on at least four websites, including our network. Allegedly, the documents contain evidence of election tampering and treason, however this is an *unverified* claim since we haven't read through the contents yet."

"Yeah," the younger of the two men said, "this is clearly a George Soros plot. Today is truly a sad day in our history."

For the second time that morning, foamy soda splashed across the carpets of the Lincoln Bedroom as the President shot out of his chair. "Why didn't anyone tell me?" he shouted; running towards his office. He stopped, winded, grabbing his chest and fighting to catch his breath. He panted and huffed for a good half-minute before he noticed someone leaning calmly against the wall nearby.

"Looks like you've finally done it," Paul Ryan said, his pointed, elfish face staring down at the President.

"Nothing's wrong. Everything will be fine."

"Not this time. You may not have noticed, but it's over. We need to run. I have a plan, but we need to go, now."

"Who's we? They can't touch me. I'm the President."

"You know after they impeach you, you would still face charges, right?"

"I'll get a bag."

oOo

"Quick, before the FBI catches up," Ryan shouted as he bolted from the helicopter across the windswept tarmac. Behind him, a clutch of people ran in a jerky, jagged series of lurches, with President Trump at the lead. The rest of the group consisted of the only people Trump thought he could trust: his daughter Ivanka, Senator Mitch McConnell, Vice-President Mike Pence, HUD Director Ben Carson (in reality, they'd just found him wandering the White House halls), Rudy Giuliani, and, god help him, Eric. *Where was Kellyanne when he needed her?*

They reached the idling plane as the first of the six helicopters touched down, and by the time Old Turtle made his way up the steps to the door the other five had landed, dotting the tarmac like insects.

"Move your asses!" Ryan screeched, pushing Benny onto the plane. On the tarmac, armored men with submachine guns poured out of their choppers shouting commands no one could hear.

"Dad," Eric said as the President began to climb, "where are we going?"

Trump turned on the stairs. "Somewhere safe until we expose Soros and whoever else is behind this," he shouted above the engine noise. "But, and I'm sorry, there isn't room on the plane for all of us."

"Course there is dad, look," Eric said, pointing at the plane with 'TRUMP' stenciled down the side. "It's a pretty big plane."

"That it is buddy, that it is." The President grabbed the cooler off his son's shoulder. "But I need you here. Since your brother got arrested, you need to look after the company. I'll leave the Secret Service guys here to help you out. I'm counting on you, Big Guy." Trump was through the door and gone before his guards or Eric could respond.

From the speeding plane they all watched the two Secret Service agents vacate the runway; and saw the younger Trump get tackled as the plane rose from the ground, leaving the country behind.

oOo

Oceans are boring.

Trump hit send and plopped the phone on his lap. The view in every direction was slate gray over dingy blue as far as the President could see. How had it come to this? And with *these* people—of all people? Giuliani was passed out in his seat, head rolled back, and mouth hinged open. Mitch was out as well, his arms crossed over his chest and head tucked down into his shoulders. With Jared in jail, Ivanka had certainly been around more often. She was sleeping now, curled in a tight ball next to him. Pence sat further back with the same placid expression as always, staring directly at Trump.

"What?" the President asked.

Pence slowly blinked and turned his focus to a window on the other side of the cabin. After a moment he said, "I wasn't given a chance to say goodbye to Mother." He continued to stare longingly out the window.

Creepy bastard.

On the screen, the talking heads were yammering. "The situation is still unfolding here. The President's departure with so many of the nation's leaders continues to raise questions."

"That's right, Tracy. We just received word that the remaining cabinet members are gathered at Camp David, sources indicate they are said to be considering invocation of the 25th amendment, which would result in turning the Presidency over to Nancy Pelosi. The NRA is threatening armed demonstrations should that occur. There are also reports of Speaker Pelosi meeting with House Leadership to consider impeachment."

"Well personally, I think the President made the right call. Look at the facts—before yesterday none of these documents existed, then *boom*! Hundreds of pages, fake pages, no validation whatsoever. Seems fishy to me. Now," he said directly to the camera, "we want your thoughts, and we'll be reading some of your responses, after the break."

"So," Trump said to Ryan once the commercials had become sufficiently boring. "Leave the country? That was your big plan? Now what? What exactly is going on?"

"Well," Ryan said, "in answer to your first question, we're headed to Crimea. To your second, they have everything."

"Everything?"

Ryan gave a sage nod, "And not just on you." He pulled his phone from his coat, "You want to see the email from Putin's staff to McConnell, he gestured to the tear streaked face of the lumpy bulge in a seat two rows back, telling him to not, under any circumstances, allow a vote for Merrick Garland to proceed? And that's just a tidbit."

"I never, not ever once, colluded with Russia. Vlad's a friend and your Bill Barr's report."

"I didn't say you did, and you might not have, but *everyone* else did for you."

"Who could do this?" Trump asked, ignoring the jab, "Who sold me out?"

"Anonymous, emailed from an unregistered private server."

"That fu—"

"It wasn't Clinton."

"Lies. Lies. Lies!." He pounded his armrest, leaving tiny fist sized impressions in the Corinthian leather. It's Fake News, Fake News. You'll see. Those documents aren't even real."

"I assure you, they're real."

"Nope, you'll see. This will all blow over. Best vindication ever, probably, in all history too, then *I'll* be the one starting investigations. I'll close the government until someone comes clean."

"You can't just..." The former Speaker of the House sighed in exasperation. "No, I'm not responsible for your stupidity any more. If you don't understand your job, that's on you."

"You can't call me stupid!" The President's face reddened. "I'm the best! Could a stupid person build a multimillion-dollar company by himself? Could they win an—"

"Oh save it," McConnell said, apparently woken by the conversation. "We're done!. You're just repeating yourself and irritating me."

"Lord knows I shouldn't irritate the Great Kentucky Tortoise."

"Funny," the old man said and lowered his head under the edge of his blanket.

"Ah, hey back there," the pilot said over the intercom, jolting Giuliani from his lumberjack grace slumber. "We're about to enter British airspace and I'm getting a transmission from the RAF you may want to hear."

"Put it on," Trump shouted over the noise in the cabin.

"Hello Mr. President," said a cheerful British voice, "and hello to everyone currently aiding and abetting you. This is Captain Daniel Brattock of her Majesty's Royal Air Force. It would seem you've found yourself in a fine pickle. Now, I would not presume to understand the plans of a man such as you. However," a gale of laughter filled the speakers "to resolve any ambiguity on whether or not the United Kingdom is willing to aid your antics, I'm calling to inform you that twelve surface-to-air missiles are primed and tracking your location as of this moment. Should you attempt to violate British airspace, other than for a brief, and uneventful flyover, we will put these warheads to use. The terms of this arrangement are non-negotiable and will not be repeated, so I hope you paid attention. Finally, on behalf of myself, the royal family, parliament, the military, and every citizen of the United Kingdom, please, do fuck off."

Trump scowled and went back to watching the television. "I didn't want to land in that shithole anyway. They treated me *very* unfairly."

"We're not," said Ryan. "But try not to start an international incident in the next few hours."

"He called me, how is it my fault?"

"Just don't engage with anyone. Keep a low profile."

The President had already stopped listening, his attention turned to the screen in his hand. Moments later, a erupted on the on the television.

Donald J. Trump @realDonaldTrump
HER MAJESTY just threatened to shoot my plane, THE PRESIDENT'S PLAIN DOWN. Allies for all of history and they try to threaten us. Pathetic!' So it looks like.....

Paul Ryan grabbed unsuccessfully for the phone. "What did I just say?!"

"Doesn't matter!" Trump stood and straightened his back, leveling himself with Ryan. "People, millions of followers, deserve to know how I'm being treated. They need to know I'm still in control."

"But you're not! All you ever manage to do is fan the flames."

"They started it!" Trump gestured with the cellphone in his hand, waving and pointing it like a remote control. "I'm the only one trying to put fires *out*."

"How, could you possibly, think th—"

From behind the President, Mitch McConnell plucked the device from Trump's hand and stepped out of the man's reach. Before Trump could finish lumbering around, he dropped the phone to the floor and stomped on it until it let out a satisfying *crunch*. "There," he said, adjusting his glasses, "I've wanted to do that for years."

"You son of a bitch. I... I'll..." a fit of coughing overtook the president.

"*You'll* not do a damn thing!" McConnell said, and turned back to his seat. "Someone should have done that years ago." He re-crossed his arms and settled back into his chair, and pulled his blanket up to his nose, his glare defiant.

Ryan retreated as another fit of coughing erupted from the President. Around the cabin, everyone was smirking at the childish display of commotion from the three men—all except Pence, who had yet to blink.

oOo

The flight over Europe continued—France repeated England's sentiment. At least as far as he was told; Trump didn't speak French because honestly, why would he want to? He sent a tweet from Ivanka's phone, which he had managed to swipe without anyone noticing, letting people know his opinion anyway: the French were not to be trusted. Real countries didn't surrender.

The land under them gave way to the gentle waves of the Black Sea, a peaceful, unbroken expanse of deep blue. Trump wasn't impressed.

"Okay," Ryan called from the back of the main cabin. "It's time. Let's get ready."

After everyone turned to look at him, Ryan held up a lumpy black bag, then gestured to the others piled at his feet. "Come on, everyone needs one."

"For what?" Trump asked.

"To get off the plane."

"We're thousands of feet in the air. We can't just get off."

"They're parachutes, Donald," Pence said, his tone matching his unmoved expression. "He means for us to jump."

"Fuck that! What's gotten into you? We're going to be landing soon."

"We aren't landing. Extradition exists, you know."

"So what, jump out and swim to our new lives as Ukrainian peasants? No thank you. I am *still* the President. Of America."

"Regardless, I've made arrangements." Ryan pointed out the window to a small white streak cutting through the water below. "We'll have a pick up."

"You really expect me—"

Ryan handed the pilot a parachute and turned to face Trump..

"Unless you can fly a plane better than you can spell, put on the fucking parachute. We're going. Now."

One by one, the occupants of the plane begrudgingly got up, shambled over, claimed their parachute, and followed Ryan below deck while he droned directions. "If you start to tumble, just spread your arms and legs wide to stabilize yourself." The President chuckled at that, thinking of the last time he was around this many people with their legs spread. "Once you've gotten control over which direction you're facing, pull the chute and hold on. You'll reach the ground just fine. Mitch, you ready?"

"Ah... well, I suppose, maybe I sho—" The rest was drowned out as Ryan pushed him out the hatch.

Next, Ryan approached the open maw of the cargo door. "Okay, you guys saw how it's done. Good luck," he said over his shoulder before vanishing into the howling air.

oOo

Upon splashing down in the Black Sea, two thoughts went through Trump's presidential head. First, that he hated the lying moron who came up with the idea of a fucking parachute, the flimsy balloon didn't help him *land* on the water, he *hit* the water, this was exactly what his doctor's bone spur diagnosis was supposed to prevent. Second, what water had the right to be so goddamned cold? Wasn't this the middle of a desert?

It took him a moment of flapping his arms about to spin around and find a yacht floating some twenty yards away. He bobbed with his head just above the surface for a moment and watched as Ryan climbed a ladder up the boat's rear deck. Did they mean for *him* to swim over there? Really? *Unbelievable.*

Twenty minutes later, the only other people to make it aboard the yacht were Ivanka, Mitch McConnell minus a pair of glasses, and Mike Pence. Of all the people, why did Pence have to be one of them? The Vice-Presidential human prototype stood on the deck with that infuriatingly blank face; his hair hadn't even moved.

When the door to the rear cabin opened, the little band of political refugees turned in unison as a woman in full military regalia came out to greet them. In one graceful, well-practiced motion Trump smoothed his hair, straightened his wet jacket, and sized the woman up; blonde, a pretty face a fairly good body, and a titillating Russian accent. President Donald Trump smiled; at least he was sure he was among friends.

With Ivanka's phone, Trump let the people know that he was finally okay.

Donald J. Trump @realDonaldTrump
I am safe. Don't believe lies and Fake News stories about me. No collusion! Nothing to Impreach. I am Your Prewsifent, now and always! #TrumptheGreat

He passed the phone back to Ivanka and scoffed at McConnell—thanks to him that would probably be his final tweet before he got a new phone.

The woman, Tatiana, led them to an indoor open lounge area in the lower deck and invited them all to relax and have a seat. Immediately, McConnell obliged, mumbling something about this being closer to what he expected as he squinted and fumbled toward a sofa. Tatiana pointed out the bar and kitchenette for everyone, then added, "Except for you Mr. President, if you'd please follow me, you're needed elsewhere." Without another word, she led Trump up a flight of stairs to a large red door where she stopped, composed herself, and knocked.

"Bring them." Came a grizzled voice from inside, and Tatiana pushed open the door. The windowless room beyond was brilliant red and gold with a massive wooden desk in the center, behind which sat the President of the Russian Federation, Vladimir Vladimirovich Putin.

oOo

"Welcome, please sit. First, let me start by clearing up any misconceptions about why you're here. Early this morning, after hearing of your predicament, I placed a call to your former colleague Paul Ryan to offer my assistance. Considering the situation, he was more than eager to accept."

"Help? I don't need help. I need to tell the great people of America that I was framed! I'm the best president they've had, and they know it—everyone knows it. Can you work with me on that?"

"Not interested. In truth, I directed you here for an explanation, nothing more."

"Explanation? Explanation of what? Crooked Hillary did this. Fake documents—well, not Hillary, she's not smart enough, I mean she was selling those kids out of a pizza place. Have you been to the pizza places in DC? They're okay but not *Yuge* like the pizzas we have in New York but now the DEMORats are probably putting fluoride in the pizzas to control people's minds, I bet that's why New York voted for Crooked Hillary. I know they rigged the election there, so she didn't actually—"

Vlad cleared his throat and the President faltered. Did this man just interrupt him? He was about to expose the entire conspiracy!

"I like people to know they have been beaten."

"I wasn't *beaten*—I won the presidency! I *won!*" Vlad smiled at him. Not the smile of a human, but that of a wolf emerging from tall grass. Trump studied the scene before him for a moment before shouting, "You released the documents!"

Putin chuckled and shook his head, "Hardly, I only recognized an opportunity and provided encouragement to someone I found sufficiently motivated. The rest," he showed teeth, "you could consider good fortune on my part."

"Well, obviously I understand what you're implying."

"Of course you don't, understanding requires one to pay attention. If you had, you might have noticed how close the threat truly was. Allow me to enlighten you." He leaned forward and pressed a button on his intercom.

Trump heard the door open behind him and soft footsteps entered the room. He locked eyes with the woman who betrayed him.

"YOU? You can't have betrayed me—you're not smart enough!"

"Miss Knavs, thank you for joining us." Putin stood as he greeted the First Lady.

Trump tensed with fury. He raised a hand to smack the stupid, gold digging broad across her self-righteous, backstabbing face when Putin appeared at her side. Instead Trump only sneered, "Melania, you bitch."

Melania's cool mask darkened. "I never wanted to be First Lady. Before any of this started, I made that perfectly clear, but you didn't listen. So, I adapted, played the part, and for years I did everything you told me. I've gone where you said, looked how you said, parroted what you told me, lived where you told me; I've lied for you, defended you, dealt with constant ridicule for your actions, all for you, all so you could golf and screw porn stars as King Trump. It's sickening, and I'm done. Done with your insanity. Done with *you*. Think of today's events as a good by. You are shit!"

Putin turned a cellphone over in his hands and said, "Now, now, we mustn't treat our guests like that." He started pecking fingers at the phone while he continued. "I'm sure he'll never really understand." Putin set the phone on the desk and turned his attention back to Trump. "As for you, I believe we've allowed you to run about long enough. You've caused a sufficient enough mess that your successor should be adequately occupied with the clean-up for a few years."

"Successor?! I'm the President of the goddamned United States. The most powerful man in the world!"

"Not anymore. But you don't need to worry; instead, consider this..." Putin slid the cellphone across the polished desktop. The phone spun a half turn and came to rest against Trump's golf-ready stomach.

Since the start of this horrible, whirlwind day Trump had watched his world fall apart piece by piece—the country he saved turned against him by lies, assets seized by the lying FBI, his company left in the hands of an imbecile, Ivanka taken away... and his wife orchestrated all of it. He immediately recognized the app open in front of him. Instinctively he reached for the phone. And stared blankly at the screen.

For years Twitter had been one of Trump's closest friends, his confidant and sounding board to inform people of his greatest ideas, and smartest observations. For all intents and purposes, Twitter had become his voice to a world begging them to listen. "No," he said. Tears sprang unbidden to his eyes. "You can't. Not that." His pleading eyes reached out to Vlad. "I'll change. I'll do whatever you want."

But now here he was, about to lose it all, looking down at a screen with a red lettered button labeled 'DEACTIVATE'.

"You have a choice Mister Trump," Putin said as Trump stared at the phone, silence broken only by an old man's struggling sobs. "You can press that button and retire to a quiet life, or be relocated to the deepest hole Siberia has to offer, where no one would hear you anyway. But choose quickly, because I'm growing tired of your company."

Hell's Angel

Robert Walton

Heaven is vast, but it does have boundaries and beyond those boundaries Chaos resides. Horned demons larger than stars lurk among nearly infinite shadows. Needless to say, it's a jungle out there, especially for small angels like me. Think butterflies flitting between Tyrannosaurs— Tyrannosaurs ravenous for tasty butterflies. Did I mention that my wings are gossamer, luminous and evanescent? Nevertheless, we angels have work to do and my current job is outside the boundaries of Heaven, though not strictly in Chaos. I'm here in Hell, or at least the entrance to Hell. It's safer for me down here—mostly safer—than out among the Tyrannosaurs.

My job is to offer last chances. God is such a softy! She relishes last chances, last second epiphanies, prodigal sons and all that, so here I am.

Ah, here comes a customer now.

"Excuse me, sir?"

A pear-shaped man with smallish eyes and voluptuous lips studies me with visible disdain. "Where's your tail?"

"I have none."

"Horns?"

"Nope."

"Aren't you a demon?"

"Quite the opposite, sir. May I offer condolences over your heart attack?"

"It was Comey's fault."

I check his last meal—three Big Macs, double fries and a Diet Coke—right. "I hope you didn't suffer greatly."

"I'm suffering now. Get out of my way."

"But, sir, these are the gates of Hell!"

The voluptuous lips purse. "Then I'm in the right place. Move."

I hold up a restraining hand. "You should know, sir, that I'm your last chance to make a deal with God!"

"I'm listening."

I look at my tablet. "You have quite a list here: belittling women, groping them, grabbing their—"

"They liked it."

"You achieved great wealth by cheating contractors, bringing false lawsuits, defrauding partners and abusing workers."

"Just business."

"This last election you demeaned, degraded and criminalized your opponent."

"Crooked Hillary? She deserved it."

"What about Putin?"

"What about him?"

"You turned our closest international friends into enemies and executed his agenda to foment anti-democratic chaos in the world."

"So?"

"But that was treason!"

"Get to the point!"

I peruse the rest of the list. "Well, there are quite a few things I didn't mention the mafia connections, human trafficking." I scan further. "And a couple more rather titillating pages."

"Tit-illating? Are you talking about Pocahontas?"

"Never mind." I scan the last page. "MS-13 was a big contributor to one of your super PACs?"

"Some very good people in that group. Cut to the chase."

"I offer you hope of reaching heaven."

"Heaven?"

"Heaven!"

"Big deal."

"But... don't you care about paradise?"

"Sure. It's one of my hotels."

"No, no—floating in the clouds, eternal bliss and all that."

"So who gets in?"

"All who seek God's mercy—the poor, the humble, the contrite."

"And the races are all mixed up?"

"There are blessed from every race, every culture."

"That's SAD!"

"Well... "

"And you think I can get in if I want?"

I nod. "If you repent of these sins and show genuine remorse for the pain you've caused."

"What's the catch? I heard it. You didn't say it, but I heard it."

"Well, you will likely serve a term in Purgatory pondering your misdeeds and then be eligible for admission to heaven." I scan yet another page. "Actually, quite a long term in purgatory."

"Out of my way!"

The rotund man pushes past me.

"But, sir, you're slated to descend to Hell's lowest circle!"

He turns. "That's where they put the bad boys?"

"And girls, too, sir."

"Yeah, yeah."

"Torquemada, Catherine de Medici, Mengele—yes, the worst of the worst."

"Hitler?"

"Him, too."

"My type of people."

The infernal gates gape wide, molten sulfur dripping from their hinges; poisonous vapor curling from caverns within. The man barges through without a twitch of discomfort.

I wave. "Adieu."

Voice distorted by heat, he calls back, "I'm on Twitter. Tweet me if you come up with a better deal."

Glowing yellow smoke erases him from view.

"Well, your hair is already orange. That may count for something with Mr. Luci."

Footsteps sounds on the stairs behind me. I turn. "Ah, President Putin, allow me to express my regrets at your recent terminal experience! The shirtless mode is much riskier with our ozone layer in tatters, no? You may be interested to hear that I was just speaking with a friend of yours. If you'll pause a moment, I'll bring up your files."

What is Hate?

Joyce Frohn

Hate is the color of...
 blood on asphalt that no one bothers to wash off.
Hate sounds like...
 machine gunfire and screams.
Hate looks like...
 the eyes of a man who doesn't want you to exist.
Hate smells like...
 the metallic odor of old blood.
Hate tastes like...
 gunpowder, floating thickly through the air.
Hate feels...
 slimy as it tries to climb into your mind.
Hate walks in the shadows, waiting for a person,
 to become one with,
to release hate into an all too ready world.

Beautocracy

Natalie Zellat Dyen

Pamela put on her black silky wig, stepped into a pair of stilettos, and headed for her job interview at the high school. *I'm a damn good teacher,* she thought. *They'd be idiots not to offer me the position.* But when she walked into the office and the interviewer greeted her with pursed lips and narrowed eyes, she knew the deck was stacked against her, despite the CV that had gotten her in the door.

"You mean my PhD and references count for nothing?" Pamela asked the interviewer, a petite blond high school principal with a kewpie doll face.

"That's not what I'm saying. But we have to weigh all the factors. And we know that students learn more from attractive teachers than unattractive ones. The research is indisputable."

The kewpie doll principal tapped her leg impatiently, but Pamela was not one to give in easily. She pulled a batch of student testimonials out of her briefcase.

"When you weigh all the factors, shouldn't you take past performance into account?" She handed the packet over to the interviewer, who glanced at the top sheet and handed it back.

"Very nice," she said condescendingly, "but we've interviewed several other candidates with PhDs and rave reviews. And all things being equal…"

All things were *not* equal. Since the Supreme Court had ruled that companies could use physical attractiveness as a consideration in their hiring practices, studies suddenly showed that beautiful people brought in more money for their employers, were more productive, and were more intelligent than their less attractive counterparts. Never mind who funded them.

At thirty-one, Pamela didn't need to be reminded of her physical shortcomings. There were official tools to do that for her. She had uploaded her most flattering photo to an attractiveness calculator app. The app compared her features to the template of the perfect face as defined by the Golden Ratio, a configuration that occurs repeatedly in nature and art and is considered to be universally pleasing to the eye.

The calculator had rendered its judgment in searing red letters: *You are ugly!* On a scale of one to ten, she'd scored a two—just one notch above "very ugly." The score was accompanied by a long list of specifics, a blistering judgment from the Almighty, a final grade of F on her permanent record.

Women using the site could get an rendition of themselves after "corrective" surgery with an automatic referral to the cosmetic surgeon sponsoring the website, confident that they were just a nip and tuck away from going to sleep a *two* and waking up a *nine* or *ten*. And all of it covered by insurance. No copays, no deductibles. Perfection on the cheap.

Many women she knew had already gone under the knife, and the rest seemed to be making plans. But not Pamela. She and her sister Alice had sworn to each other that they'd never give in to the "beautocracy," a term Pamela had coined in her dissertation. Alice liked to say that their rough oyster-shell exteriors were nothing more than protective covers for the precious pearls hidden inside.

Attractiveness had always been a valued commodity, but now women were paying a penalty for not living up to the new expectations. It was becoming harder—often dangerous—for women who looked like her to walk the streets. Which is why she had worn stilettos and covered her frizzy hair with a wig for this interview.

But despite Pamela's two best features—great legs and a photogenic smile—the principal simply stood and crossed her arms, effectively ending the interview.

"So that's it?" Pamela said angrily, stuffing the folder back into her briefcase. When she stood, she was several inches taller than the little Barbie, which gave her a fleeting sense of superiority. She strode to the door, then stopped.

"Your loss. I have more to offer than a dozen air-headed... Oh, hell. Never mind." She slammed the door behind her.

Fueled by anger and frustration, Pamela strode briskly toward the bus stop, brushing past women swathed in gauze wound around necks, stretched over chins and foreheads, wearing their bandages as casually as accessories. She barely missed bumping into a woman who had stopped to admire herself in a store window, gazing down at her chest in awe, as if her enhanced breasts were shiny new toys. *The female body as playground.*

Pamela stopped short when she spotted two men in identical black leather jackets up ahead. The monster-face insignias embossed on their jackets and the black leather boots and aviator glasses identified them as self-styled "streetcleaners" on the prowl for "beasties". That was the new catchword for women like her. Pamela turned and race-walked in the opposite direction, her high heels tack-tacking against the pavement. Damn stilettos had become a de facto fashion standard, and anyone wearing heels lower than three inches faced ridicule—or worse. She thought it ironic that she needed high heels to maintain a low profile.

Pamela was breathing hard by the time she caught up with a group of young girls, their heads buried in their electronic devices, looking up periodically to communicate with each other. Their long silky hair bounced as they strode confidently in their high heels, some with bandages. According to the new conventional wisdom, it was never too early to get started on the road to perfection. Pamela followed close behind on the chance that someone in the crowd might come to her aid if the vigilantes decided to rough her up. Not likely. People had become less tolerant of beasties once they no longer had to pay for plastic surgery. *If you're still a beastie, it's your own damn fault.* She took a quick look behind her. No leather jackets in sight.

Pamela's anger was still burning white hot when she got to her apartment, so she called her sister. Alice had been the youngest member of the House of Representatives until being voted out in the last election. She'd been enormously popular—a passionate advocate for her constituents and a tireless spokesperson for women's rights—until the beauty cult got a stranglehold on the neck of the American public. Pamela had watched the televised debate, cringing when Alice's opponent pointed a finger and said, "Look at her. Why would anyone vote for someone with a face like that?" A majority of her constituents apparently agreed, because she lost the election.

"What are you planning to do, now that you can't teach?" Alice asked.

"Beats me." Pamela paused. "I'm sure I'll find something. Otherwise I'll have to leave Philly." Silence.

"I'm not sure I can stay in Virginia either."

"Where would you go?"

"Oregon," said Alice. She explained how she was working with a group of fellow activists to set up a sanctuary city in Portland for women like them. It was going to take a few months to get everything set up, then Pamela could join her.

"I'll find something for now," said Pamela, and the call ended. It wouldn't be easy, companies were demanding beauty for everything, even research positions and back-office jobs, claiming that the presence of unattractive women had a negative effect on the morale of co-workers.

Whenever her resolve flagged, Pamela would break out the family photo album to remind herself why she stayed the course. Pamela was descended from a line of fighters, from Alice Paul to her grandmother and mother, all of whom had been leaders in the women's movement. This was her family. This is what they looked like. This is what *she* looked like, and she was proud to be one of them. Adopting a new face would be a betrayal. And as a student of history and sociology, Pamela knew the importance of continuity and the price one paid for tearing down the past.

oOo

Eventually Pamela found work as a part-time fact-checker. It was an on-line gig that barely paid the rent, even for her cheap third-floor walkup in a down-at-the-heels townhouse complex in Northeast Philadelphia. But if she could just hang in for a few more months, she'd be able to leave Philly and join the resistance. The movement seemed to be growing, albeit slowly. There were stories of brave women who spoke out at the risk of public humiliation, planned strategies to confront Congress, and established safe houses around the country. The resisters called themselves the WYSIWYGs (What You See Is What You Get), pronounced "wizzywig." It was an acronym that was coined in the early days of word processing, and the name said it all.

After finishing her last assignment of the day, Pamela made a list of things she'd forgotten to order online as the TV droned in the background. Something about the Streetcleaners being granted official status under the umbrella of the Department of Health and Human Services. To her they were still goon squads, and she hoped she wouldn't encounter any on her way to the pharmacy.

Bewigged and dressed in a heavy coat and scarf, she made her way carefully along snow-covered sidewalks to the pharmacy, her pace slowed by her stiletto boots. Once inside, she checked for customers before venturing down one of the aisles. Besides the cashier and the pharmacist, she appeared to be the only one there.

Pamela located the tampons she needed at the end of an aisle stocked with contraceptives, erectile dysfunction drugs, and morning-after pills. After the President had been overheard saying, "We'd all be safer if every man could get laid on a regular basis (hey I was only joking)," researchers took it seriously and released studies that identified sexual frustration as a primary cause of violence. After that, Congress voted to make both Viagra and birth control available over the counter. Who said Congress didn't believe in science? Then they'd legalized prostitution and, after considerable debate, had voted to make abortion completely legal, for registered prostitutes, all for the sake of national security and economic growth.

The heat in the store was cranked up to equatorial levels, so she unzipped her overcoat and unwrapped the scarf that covered the lower half of her face. She passed the cosmetics aisle on the way to the cashier, and as she reached down for a tube of lipstick, she caught the movement of a dark figure out of the corner of her eye—a man in a black leather jacket, gloves, boots, and black knit cap. Maybe he'd turn at the cross aisle. No such luck; he was headed toward her.

The heavy scent of exotic perfumes in the next aisle hung heavy as tropical vines, sweat trickled down her neck and between her breasts, and her heart pounded a jungle beat. Now the stranger was standing next to her. He raised his gloved hand, and Pamela braced for a slap, a shove, a grab. Instead, he pulled off his hat, releasing a cascade of blond hair. Not a he. A she. Pamela's relief was tempered by the thought that women could sometimes be as cruel as men.

"Damn, it's hot in here," said the blonde.

Unable to speak, Pamela nodded.

"Know where the tampons are?"

Pamela giggled at the unexpected question. "Over there." She giggled again.

The blonde gave her a look, shook her head slowly, and walked away.

Pamela paid and walked outside. Though her escape to Portland was still months away, the possibility of a brighter future lightened her step. She stood tall, taking long, confident strides, remembering how it felt to be normal. Until she heard the voice behind her.

"Think you're hot stuff strutting like a model, Beastie?"

The voice was male but high-pitched, like an adolescent on the cusp of manhood. She couldn't see his face, as he encircled her waist from behind with one leather-clad arm and covered her mouth with his other hand, cutting her off mid-scream. Pamela tried to shake herself free but couldn't loosen his vise-like grip. Definitely not an adolescent.

Her assailant dragged her down the deserted sidewalk to a narrow alley between two blocks of brick townhouses. The alley was dark, the only light coming from a couple of windows on either side. Overflowing trash cans and black plastic trash bags lined one side of the narrow path, saturating the air with the stench of rotting garbage. Her attacker jerked her around and slammed her against the rough brick wall.

Pam tried to grab the lid of a metal trash can to defend herself, but it slipped from her grasp, hitting the ground like a cymbal, the sound playing encores down the narrow pathway. Startled, her assailant lifted his hand from her mouth, and she screamed.

"Do that again, Beastie, and I'll kill you," he said, the light from an overhead window casting ghostly shadows on a sharp-featured, ferret-like face that was already distorted by rage. He pressed the point of a knife against her throat and she froze. With his free hand, he unzipped her jacket.

"Damn, Beastie," he said, gripping one of her breasts through the thin material of her t-shirt. "Nothing to hold on to." She screamed again, and he pressed the knife deeper into her neck, drawing blood. "I'll teach you to go out looking like this."

A window above them opened, and a man yelled. "What the hell's goin' on down there? Get off my property or I'll call the cops."

"Help!" she screamed, but the man had already slammed the window shut.

Her attacker fumbled with the zipper of his jeans, cursing when it got stuck. The guy was at least a foot taller than she was and built like a linebacker. His unlikely soprano voice would have provided comic relief under other circumstances. As frightened as she was, she was tempted to insult his manhood, but he'd undoubtedly finish the job on her neck if she did. His zipper was down, and he was reaching inside his pants when a police siren rang out, ear-splittingly loud as if the car were right there in the alley. Her attacker froze, then laughed when the theme song of a well-known police procedural sounded though an open window above them.

The guy will probably kill me after he... after he... Stop! This is no time to start playing the helpless female. Not after all that strength training and those self-defense classes. No way this rodent-faced shit is going to do this to me. If she remained calm and thought it through, she could get the better of him. She had to. Weapons? No, she'd forgotten to carry her key ring with keys dangling to whack her assailant across the face. What else? Hard to think while her feet were going numb in the flimsy stiletto boots. Stiletto boots! She was wearing her weapons. Pamela had practiced disabling mock assailants with the surprise and pain of a high heel jammed into the top of a foot. She'd have to drive it home on the first try.

Though her attacker's private parts were now exposed, she was more concerned with his footwear. If he was wearing heavy boots, she'd be screwed in more ways than one. Mustering all her energy, she rammed a stiletto heel into his foot, and he let out a banshee scream. Before he could bend all the way over to nurse his injured foot, she jammed a knee into his crotch for good measure. Then she ran down the alley, setting trash cans clattering like angry timpani. Before she reached the street, her heel hit something slippery, but she managed to stay upright. She risked a quick look behind her. The would-be rapist was still tending to his injured parts. She couldn't risk another fall, so she pulled off her boots and ran in stocking feet. The initial shock was soon replaced by numbness, as if she were running on wooden blocks, but somehow she was able to make it home

Pamela sat on the edge of the tub and ran warm water over her feet until the feeling returned, then filled the tub with hot water and got in. She closed her eyes and imagined what would happen if she went to the police, took her attacker to court, and made him pay. But she knew how that would play out. They'd laugh at her, insist it couldn't have happened because she was so coyote ugly, no one would want to rape the likes of her. For all she knew, "coyote ugly" was now a legitimate defense for rapists. Hopefully, that wouldn't be the case in Portland.

oOo

On the day of her departure, Pamela swathed her head in gauze, texted her sister and left a voicemail message. She hadn't been able to contact Alice for the last couple of days, but since they'd already firmed up the date and time of her arrival, there was really no need. Pamela called a car service to take her to Thirtieth Street Station, where she'd hop a train to the airport. Then she closed her apartment door for the last time.

When the car turned off I95 and headed across town, Pamela bade silent goodbyes to the landmarks that had been fixtures in her life—Independence Hall, the Academy of Music—but her heart zig-zagged in her chest when they stopped for a red light in front of the new Franklin Clinic. Once they moved past, she breathed easier knowing her journey wouldn't end there. She couldn't bear to think about what they did to women in places like that.

Thirtieth Street Station, a neoclassical style building dominated by massive Corinthian columns, was her gateway to freedom, though today she found the exterior strangely off-putting. But the interior was welcoming despite the presence of goon squads and crowds of people, any one of whom could blow her cover. There was something almost spiritual about the warm light filtering through cathedral-like windows and blessing the people below, announcements echoing as incomprehensibly as murmured prayers, and art deco chandeliers hanging like giant paper lanterns from an intricately patterned ceiling. Lost in a sea of fellow travelers, many of them sporting bandages like hers, she pictured the trains beneath her, carrying passengers in all directions, carrying her to freedom. What was it about this place that felt so welcoming? Then it came to her. The building was a metaphor. An off-putting façade hiding a complex—dare she say beautiful—interior. The pearl in the oyster shell.

When she got to the airport Pamela texted her sister and called again. Still no answer. But she was too excited to worry, and when the plane took off, Pamela's heart soared in tandem with the engines. Only a few more hours and she'd be reunited with her sister. Her *twin* sister. Her mirror image. The two would act with one mind as they always had, following in the footsteps of the family matriarchs. Pamela turned her head toward the window and put on a sleep mask. In spite of the media's blind eye and the President's proposed bill to impose sanctions on sanctuary cities, she imagined the resistance movement steadily growing, supported by a small but vocal network of churches that had been fighting for them. And when Pamela finally dozed, lulled by the steady drone of the engines, she dreamed of a massive choir of resisters singing the *Hallelujah Chorus* at Thirtieth Street Station.

oOo

Security at Portland International was tighter than what she'd encountered in Philly. When a guard questioned her, scrutinizing her face and her ID, she responded with a laugh. "Looks like I need new a ID." He smiled and let her go, but as she walked to the ground transportation counter, she looked back and saw him pick up his cell phone. *Don't be paranoid. Three-quarters of the people at this airport are on cell phones at this very moment.*

After arranging for a car, Pamela went outside to wait. *I'm so close.* When the driver signaled her to get in, she gave him her sister's address and got into the back seat. *So close! What a relief to be... almost home.* She closed her eyes and drifted off. When she awakened with a start, she checked the time. Twenty minutes had elapsed. Her sister lived close to the airport, but the ride seemed to be taking a long time. And now they were driving down city streets. Her sister lived in the burbs. This wasn't right.

"Stop the car. Let me out." The driver didn't turn around. When they stopped for a red light, she tried the door, but it was locked.

"Let me out," she screamed. No response.

They pulled up to a sprawling, glass-clad building and the driver cut the engine. The sign over the door read Portland Rejuvenation Clinic. Two leather-jacketed goons locked arms with her and walked her inside. One of them stayed with her as they checked her in, a process that took a while because she struggled. They had to press her index finger to the scanner three times before it registered her fingerprint. The woman at the desk must have encountered her share of reluctant patients, as she didn't appear the least bit concerned.

Under the watchful eyes of the goons, Pamela sat down on one of the few empty chairs. With the exception of a couple of anxious faces among the women filling the waiting room, most of them seemed happy to be there. The soft blue-gray walls were dotted with artistically composed portraits of women with perfect faces. Other than differences in skin tone and hair color all the women looked pretty much alike. A plaque on the wall read: *Ask at the desk to see the "before" photos.*

Alice *had* to get her out of there. Pamela reached for her cell phone and dropped it. *Calm down.* She took a deep breath and quickly scanned the room. No one was looking at her. With shaking hands, she pressed her sister's number. *Please pick up.* She heard the familiar voicemail greeting and waited for the beep. Damn. "*Please* Allie, pick up. They've taken me to a clinic downtown. They're going to—"

Her sister's voice broke in. "Oh, Pammy. I'm so sorry. I didn't mean for this to happen. Hang in and I'll be there." Thank God. Her sister would take care of her.

A statuesque woman in a tight white uniform towered over her. "Don't worry dear. Everything's going to be okay. Just a few forms to fill out." She handed Pamela a tablet. "Bring it to the front desk when you're done, and I'll escort you in."

Was this the form that let women opt out? The Supreme Court had ruled that what she was about to undergo was legal, but it was unconstitutional to force women to do something like that without their consent. So they'd come up with a workaround: A women could refuse "treatment" but she'd be charged an opt-out fee that was steep enough to bankrupt all but the super-rich. The online forms in front of her were strictly medical, so apparently opting out was no longer an option.

Still, Pamela breathed a little easier knowing her sister was on her way. Allie would save her. Get her out before they strapped her to a bed, anesthetized her, and carved her a new face and body; before they did a pregnancy test and, if the result was positive, performed an abortion; before they tied her tubes, since there was a high probability that the offspring of a beastie would be another beastie, no matter how much exterior work they did on the mother; before she woke up a stranger with a set of new breasts and a face that was no longer her own. And she'd be sterile.

A handsome doctor with sympathetic eyes came to fetch her. The clinic was set up like a hospital emergency department with curtained rooms surrounding a central station. The doctor led her into one of the rooms and strapped her to the bed with leather restraints. "I'm sorry," he said, "but you know how this works."

She struggled against the restraints.

"I'm sorry," he said again, tightening the straps.

"No," she cried, her wrists chafing as she pulled against the unforgiving leather. "No, please." But he was gone. "Please," she whimpered to the empty room. She looked around at the machines, the boxes of bandages and metal objects that would be used to carve her up.

She was alone with only photographs of beautiful women to keep her company. The sign above them read: *One of these can be you.* A collection of adorable baby pictures hung on the side wall under a sign that read: *One of these can be yours.* Adoption was available for ex-beasties who wanted children. A paternalistic Congress had ruled that motherhood was a sacred right and should be available to all women, including beasties. Sterilized women could choose from a catalogue of naturally beautiful surrogates impregnated with the sperm of carefully selected men. Surrogates and sperm donors were paid big bucks to produce smart, beautiful children, so that beasties could be granted the privilege of motherhood.

The hum of activity on the other side of the curtain was broken by the occasional raised voice and the periodic click-click of stilettos against tile. *Please Allie, hurry!*

A nurse pulled the curtain. "This'll calm you down, honey." She jabbed a needle in Pamela's arm. The nurse's shrill voice was as reassuring as metal on metal. As a drug-induced warmth suffused her body, Pamela heard her sister's voice in the hall.

"Allie," she cried, but it came out a hoarse whisper. The curtain opened and a woman walked in. A woman with long legs, sleek black hair, and perfect features. A nurse? Something about the eyes. Then the stranger spoke. It was her sister's voice—the voice she knew as well as her own. Her sister's voice coming from that alien body.

"I'm so sorry, Pamela. I wanted to tell you before you got here, but I didn't have the heart. I fought with everything I had, but people refused to listen. They were put off by my looks."

Our looks.

"No one believes anything coming from the mouth of a beastie anymore. So..."

Pamela's mind was fuzzy. Maybe she was hallucinating. No, this was all too real. It took all her energy to form the question, "Did they... make you... do it?"

Her sister's eyes were dissolving in sorrow. "No, they didn't force me. I just realized I could accomplish more if I... tweaked my exterior. They even promised me a job as a legislative aide for a state senator if I just fixed myself up. They said I'd be in a better position to advocate for women's rights as an insider rather than an outsider. And you can help me after you—"

"But I don't want to..." Pamela tried to fight the drug, but it was no use.

A tear traced a path down her cheek, a mirror image of the tear that ran down her sister's face before it shimmered, blurred, and disappeared.

Kurt Newton

Alien Tweetstorm Apocalypse

Kurt Newton

It was a simple flap of wings
that ushered in a storm,
diplomacy reduced to 144 characters,
what could possibly go wrong?

YOU'RE ON NOTICE! shouted from afar
from one dictator to another,
a tactical humiliation designed to curb
nuclear proliferation, or at least that was the plan.

Until a tweet was fired back
in a language not seen since the Pharaohs,
a whodunit on a global scale,
was it Syria? China? Russia? Iran?

Tweet accusations flew,
followed by tweet denials and tweet threats,
tweet tensions grew as the strange tweets continued,
until there was but one response left.

And the aliens watched
from their long-distance view,
as the missiles were launched and the blue planet
lit up like an electrical storm.

The transmission they sent
was one of peace and reunion,
but now the homecoming will have to wait
a few hundred years more.

I, Apparatchik

Philip Brian Hall

Boris Nikolayevich has eyes like saucers. Normally. So when he staggered into my Lubyanka office with eyes as big as saucepan lids, clutching his chest like he was suffering a heart attack, I suspected something might be wrong.

"Bad news, Leonid Alexeyevitch," he gasped. "The Putin VI robot is malfunctioning!"

"Sit down Boris," I said. I'd no idea what he was talking about, but we are always told we must be seen to empathize with our staff. I invariably follow orders; it's healthier, assuming you don't care for polonium-flavored tea. "Remind me again which one is Putin VI?"

"The cheap one we'd kept in reserve, you know, so The Boss can make the first human landing on Mars just before the Americans, whenever they decide to try," Boris said.

"Ah yes." I nodded. "For a moment there you had me worried. I thought you meant the expensive one we used for all those wilderness appearances, like when The Boss flew a hang-glider to lead the annual migration of Siberian cranes."

"We actually needed three robots for that one in the end, Leonid," Boris reminded me. "Putin I, II and III. The first two went off course and we had to get the Air Force to shoot them down before they reached China. Off-camera of course."

"Of course!" I said. "Now I remember. Then there was that waterproof one, wasn't there? For when The Boss made the sensational archaeological discovery during his five-minute scuba-dive in the Black Sea."

"Putin IV," said Boris. "It's completely sealed in rubber though; not much use for anything else."

"Yes, yes, I remember. Those specialized robots cost us so much money, I even had to chip in a few thousand rubles myself. That was why we had to economize with the cheap

Putin VI for the Mars landing, wasn't it? But Boris, it's all right. No-one expects high-quality pictures from space."

"They do expect high-quality departure pictures from the Baikonur Cosmodrome!" Boris wailed. "And that could be a problem."

"Why's that, Boris?"

"Because Putin VI has already climbed into the command module and refuses to get out!"

"No! Does it say why?"

"It's jealous. It says Putin V got too much press coverage for its bare-chested horse-riding. It insists on its right to do a bare-chested landing on Mars."

"That's ridiculous! If it doesn't wear a space-suit everyone will smell a rat. We don't want them suspecting The Boss's appearances might be faked!"

"Well, I don't know, Leonid. That might be an improvement on what they think right now."

"What's that?" I demanded, flashing him an angry look.

"You hadn't heard Putin V's bare-chested fishing expedition didn't go down so well?" he mumbled awkwardly. "The Western press spotted we'd left the plastic wrapper on the handle of the fishing-rod. I'm really sorry, Leonid. I mean, how am I supposed to know every last detail about fishing?"

Boris paused, wondering if he'd said too much. I just smiled for the CCTV. Let careless talk cost other lives; it's not going to happen to me.

"No, it's much worse than that," Boris continued. "We didn't figure Putin VI would need the same finely-sculpted torso Putin V has because it would always be wearing a space suit, you remember? That was one of our economy measures."

"You mean Putin VI doesn't have a finely-sculpted torso?"

"In a way, Leonid. Actually it doesn't have a torso at all, just a sort of balloon to keep the suit inflated."

"That's bad. We can't have people thinking The Boss is a balloon!"

"Leonid, you still don't get it." Boris shook his head desperately. "Air pressure is much lower on Mars. Putin VI needs the suit to stop the balloon expanding so much it explodes!"

"Ah. You're right, Boris, Putin exploding live on-camera would really not be good."

"How about we send Putin V to Mars as well?" Boris suggested hopefully. "It can do the departure shots; they can both do the landing and Putin VI can explode off-camera?"

"Idiot. It takes years to get to Mars and back. We'll be announcing The Boss invented and piloted a special fusion-powered rocket that can go to Mars and back in a week, remember?"

"Ah, yes, I'd forgotten."

"But that means we need robots for all those years of special appearances while the Mars rocket's away, even supposing we could ever get the robots *back* from Mars, which we probably couldn't."

"We'd still have Putins III and IV," he pointed out.

"One's a flier and one's a swimmer, right? They're no use for close-up contact. Who's going to show the Russian Judo team how to do all the difficult throws before the next Olympics?"

"We could get ourselves banned from the Olympics for drug violations again," Boris suggested helpfully.

"Okay, so who's going to do the deep dive to discover the oil traces we've planted in our newly-extended Arctic waters?"

"Well, Putin IV could probably do that. It's still pretty waterproof. As long as it doesn't buckle under the pressure at that depth of course."

"Oh yes?" I glared at him. "So we risk one Putin exploding and another Putin being crushed? And who's going to attend the Summit Meeting with President Trump? Answer me that!"

"I don't know." Boris wriggled nervously in his chair. "Putin III maybe? You think Trump would notice he was talking to a robot in a flight suit?"

"I've no idea what Trump might do from one day to the next," I conceded. "I suspect he doesn't even know himself. But I can't take the risk."

"But surely, Leonid, Trump wouldn't let the cat out of the bag anyway, not after we helped get him elected."

"You think? He'd probably get up, walk around the table and pull Putin III's head off! 'Look at this,' he'd say. 'Now who's got weak hands, hey? And can anyone seriously suggest I'd collude with this goddamn machine?'"

"You are quite certain the story about Trump being a robot himself isn't true, Leonid?"

"Fake news, Boris. I made it up myself."

"But, Leonid," he wheedled, "maybe you accidentally told the truth? Did you ever consider that?"

"There's a first time for everything, I guess, but I can't take that risk either." I may have smiled a little. "Though, come to think of it, it would be really funny if the Americans were being led by a robot, wouldn't you say, Boris?"

"No, Leonid, what I mean is, surely Trump wouldn't pull the head off our robot if he was a robot himself!"

"How do I know, Boris? It might depend whether the Trump robot was programmed by the Republicans to beat the Democrats or by the Democrats to discredit the Republicans. Who could possibly tell?"

"Well, exactly, Leonid. You see, that's why I thought he might be one of ours. But getting back to the Putin robots, I don't suppose there's any way we can afford to build another one?"

"You want to use the profits you made from privatizing the State Gas Company?" I asked.

"Not really."

"There you are then. There's no money."

"Well, look," he said. "I mean, I don't normally like to suggest extravagant ideas, Leonid, but in an emergency like this, don't you think you could prevail on The Boss actually to do some of his appearances himself?"

"Are you crazy? Don't you know anything?"

"What don't I know, Leonid?"

"Putin's been dead for years, Boris, just like Brezhnev."

"You mean..."

"Exactly, Boris. Our robots are all that stands between us and a dreadful fate for Mother Russia."

"What fate's that, Leonid?" He turned chalk white. "You surely don't mean we might have to land real people on Mars?"

"Idiot!" I shuddered. "I mean we might actually have to *elect* a real person!"

Alternative Truth III: ENDGAME

Democralypse

Bruce Golden

They shoved him into the room, hands bound behind him, and forced him onto a cold metal chair. He lost his balance and someone he couldn't see grabbed him and jerked him upright. Before he could orient himself, the door shut, leaving him alone and in total darkness.

What was going on? What did he do? His only attempt to question the men who grabbed him had been met by a curse and a stinging backhand. Why were they so angry? He hadn't done anything. Why had they taken him? Was he under arrest? No one had said anything to him. They'd just stared at him with loathing.

He'd been at home, watching television—watching the president's address. He'd rushed home to see it, hoping he wouldn't miss anything. He remembered being relieved to be home in time.

Halfway through the speech, a loud banging shook his door. A voice shouted something he couldn't make out, and before he could even think to react, his door burst open, splinters of wood showering him like shrapnel.

"On the floor! On the floor!" Overlapping voices screamed at him as a flurry of uniformed men and women rushed into his apartment, their weapons threatening, their expressions invisible behind opaque face shields.

Shock had welded George to his chair. He hadn't even time to consider responding to their demands when two of the intruders yanked him from his seat and slammed him face-first onto the floor. The impact stunned him, so he barely felt the handcuffs as they squeezed his wrists. Moments later he was hauled outside under the accusing stares of his neighbors, only vaguely aware of the search-and-destroy whirlwind laying waste to his home.

Now, waiting in the dark, he'd lost track of time. He almost called out, but thought better of it. He should wait calmly. He should cooperate. Everything would be straightened out. He hadn't done anything.

Just as he realized he was going to have to relieve himself soon, several ceiling-mounted lights burst into brightness. Momentarily blinded, he heard the door open. Someone walked in.

"Where are your shoes?"

"My shoes?"

So much had happened he hadn't even considered that all he had on his feet were socks.

"What's a matter, don't you believe in shoes?" asked a second voice.

"No—I mean yes, of course I—"

"Is it some kind of cult thing? Some religious perversion?"

"What are you talking about?"

"We're talking about shoes, George. Don't you wear shoes? You got some kind of shoe phobia?"

He could see well enough now to make out two distinct figures. One was wearing a tan jacket and tie, the other a white shirt with sleeves rolled up. The latter fellow was a hulking brute with a scowl stamped on his face. In contrast, his partner seemed nonchalant.

George didn't recognize either of them, and he saw nothing in the bare room that would tell him where he was. All he saw beyond the light's glare was an empty chair positioned across from him, and a camera mounted high in the corner.

"Who are you? What's going on?"

"We'll ask questions here, Georgie," said the big fellow. "George McGrath... is that your real name?"

"Of course."

"What kind of name is that? Sounds Irish-Catholic to me. Or maybe Scottish. Are you a kilt-wearing Scotsman, Georgie?"

"No, no, I'm an American—a good American."

"So why don't you wear shoes, George?" asked the one in the jacket, examining his fingernails.

"I do—I do wear shoes. It's just that when—"

"What kind of shoes do you like, George? Do you like loafers, George? Brown loafers or black ones? Or do you like shoes you can tie up?"

"What? I don't understand what this is about."

George tried to swallow, but his mouth was dry. The big guy whirled around and thrust his face up close enough to give George a rancid whiff of sausage.

"Do you pick your toes, Georgie? What do you do with the toe jam, Georgie?"

"I don't do anything with it."

"Come on, George." It was the other one now. The way they were both at him, he didn't know who to look at. "We all get our fingers into some toe jam every now and again. There's nothing wrong with that. The question is, what do you do with it, George?"

"I don't—"

"Tell us about your fetishes, George. What kinds of things do you like?"

"I don't have any fetishes." The pressure on his bladder was becoming painful.

"Come on, George. We've all got our little quirks. Tell us what you like. Tell us about your peculiar appetites."

"I, uhh... I don't have any."

Without warning the brute roared in frustrated rage and smashed his forearm against the bare wall. George twitched involuntarily. The big man glared at him and stalked across the room. His partner eyed him, shaking his head, and then turned to George.

"Give it up, George. We know all about you. What we're really concerned about are the unknowns—the things we don't know we don't know. That's what we want you to tell us about, George."

"I... uh... I don't know what you're talking about."

What could he have done? What were they getting at? George couldn't think of anything. He hadn't done anything. All he'd done was the same thing he did every day. He thought back to when he'd gotten off work. He remembered being relieved when he reached the tram before it left the station. He was so relieved that, for once, it didn't bother him he had to stand, packed in elbow to elbow with his fellow passengers. What *had* concerned him was he didn't know whose elbows he was rubbing.

Who was standing behind him? What kind of person was the dour-faced woman next to him wearing a print dress and holding a big basket purse that kept jouncing against his thigh? Was she a party member? A subversive? A mother grieving for a son lost in battle?

On the panel above him was a familiar poster—the one with New Glory waving in an imagined breeze, and a Continental soldier, braced by his musket, reminding citizens to "Buy Patriot Bonds." The sight of it encouraged him to stand straight. His chest filled proudly and he reached up to touch the New Glory pin on his collar—the one that had come when he'd purchased his own bond.

Mounted next to the poster was a standard security cam. Its presence soothed him. It was comforting to know you could be seen almost everywhere you went. George turned to make certain the camera lens could focus on his pin.

He spotted a screen in the tram, and though the audio levels were low, the sound reverberated up and down the carriage. If he listened closely he could make out the words.

"...a charge of treason in a closed proceeding. Dr. Leonard Jefferson faces life in prison for, among other disloyal acts, ranting against public policy while on a speaking tour at the University of the Republic in New Haven, and referring to President Anwell as a 'despot.' Excerpts from the secret court will be released after evaluation by the National Security Agency."

George didn't know exactly what a "despot" was, but he knew it wasn't something you called the president. Obviously this Jefferson fellow wasn't a true citizen. No doubt he had ties to any number of subversive factions.

As he exited the tram, George saw two men on either side examining face after face. They wore no uniforms nor any other official insignias, which led George to believe they were Homeguard. They had that look, and lately they'd been prowling the tram station.

Suddenly, they took hold of a disembarking passenger and said something George couldn't hear. He strained to get a good look at the man before they hustled him away. Dark eyes, puffy cheeks, weak chin, ragged haircut... yes, George was sure the man was an Episcopalian. The thought made him shudder. Episcopalians were known carriers of UMV, and this fellow had been in the same tram car as George.

Yet hadn't he heard the Upper Mississippi Virus had been contained? Maybe the fellow was just another exposed homosexual being taken to the reservation. The weak chin certainly fit. Come to think of it, his eyebrows looked trimmed as well. That was probably it. No reason for him to start worrying over nothing. He looked away. It wasn't his business.

He was halfway home when he came to an unexpected assemblage along the roadway. He cursed them all under his breath as he pushed through, and then saw why they were there. Coming down the street was a phalanx of military vehicles. Each one was packed with troops returning, no doubt, from Finland, where their pacification of the radical leftist regime and restoration of democracy had been a success.

As the first group of soldiers motored by, George drew up rigidly and saluted, his thumb against his chest, right hand steadfast, perpendicular to his heart. The sight of New Glory, its stripes and lone star waving staunchly from the rear of each vehicle, filled him with pride. The United Republic of America had triumphed once more, and the world was a safer place because of it.

He searched the soldiers' faces for smiles of victory, but saw only dull eyes and blank expressions. They must be exhausted thought George, which only prompted him to hold his salute that much firmer. Someone near him mumbled "God bless America." He nodded his head in silent agreement, then observed, not ten feet away from him, a teenage couple canoodling there on the street, oblivious to the parade of American military might. The disrespect infuriated him.

"You there!" he declared in a tone that demanded attention. "Eyes front. Stand up straight. Show some respect." George narrowed his eyes with stern regard, gesturing toward the progression of troops.

The lanky, thin-lipped boy stared at him, but he and his girlfriend turned to face the parade. Still they didn't salute. However, George was satisfied he'd gotten their attention. Instead of saying anything else, he committed their faces to memory. Probably Oregonians from the look of them—maybe even Californians. That would explain it.

A modest sense of accomplishment had bolstered him then, even though he'd only done what any good American would. It was a small thing, but also one that had likely been captured by street security cams. Maybe he'd receive a notation of recognition from the party. Or maybe not. It didn't matter. It just felt good to belong.

But he didn't belong here. Not here in this room with lights glaring in his face, a camera bearing down on him, and these men questioning him as if he were some kind of... some kind of what? Had those teenagers concocted something? Had they borne witness against him?

The smallish interrogator scratched his head as if he needed to take a different tact. "Tell us about your dreams, George. Everybody dreams. What kinds of things do you dream about?"

"I... I don't know. I guess I dream about different things. I don't usually remember my dreams."

"Do you masturbate, George?"

"Do I *what*?"

"You heard me. Do you, George? Do you play with yourself? What do you think about when—?"

The door to the tiny room opened, cutting off the question. A woman wearing a gray pinstriped suit and carrying an oversized pad entered. The pad's screen was lit, but George couldn't see what was on it. The woman sat in the empty chair. The two men remained standing, deferring to her.

"George McGrath," she said, reading it off her pad, but ignoring him. "Yes, I've got your complete record here."

George took a breath and braced himself.

"Why am I here? Who are you people? Police? Homeguard security? I'm a good American. I've got a right to know why I'm here."

"I thought you were a good American, George," said the smaller fellow. "A good American, a *patriotic* American, wouldn't ask, wouldn't cry about his *rights*. He would just cooperate."

"I'm trying to cooperate. I just don't understand."

George strained to think back. What could he have done? He remembered walking home, sidestepping a pile of uncollected refuse, and feeling something brittle and sticky *crunch* under his shoe. He'd wiped the remnants against a broken chunk of concrete. One had to be careful where one stepped these days, what with city services being cut back to support the national security effort. Even his own building was somewhat dilapidated, though it had hot water twice a day. That was more than some places, or so he'd heard. Dreary as it was, it was good enough for him, and all he could afford.

He'd trudged up the bleak steps, oblivious to the ever-present smell of mold and boiling rice. Fumbling with his key he saw the old black woman across the hall crack her door and eye him suspiciously, secure behind her double chains. He returned her stare in kind before closing his own door behind him. He didn't like the way that woman looked at him. He'd always wondered about her. Maybe he should prompt a background check. It couldn't hurt.

He glanced at the solitary family photo which adorned his dresser. His father had doted on his two older brothers. And why not? They were the kind of sons every father wanted. When they'd both joined the Marines, his father had been so proud. He'd bragged to everyone until... until the day they were both killed in the same skirmish. It had been seven years now since the Liberian Pacification. The mission proved to be a success, eventually, but it had left his father bitter.

George had tried to enlist as soon as he was old enough, hoping to fill the void left by his older brothers, and maybe, finally, gain his father's approval. But even that wasn't to be. A childhood bout with rheumatic fever had left his heart valves thick with scar tissue. Induction doctors rejected him on medical grounds—unfit for duty to his country. There were times, even now, he lamented that he'd never been allowed to serve—never been allowed to join.

"Georgie says he doesn't have any fetishes," the big guy said, addressing the woman.

"I heard," she responded. Her expression was noncommittal, but George sensed stern disapproval behind the chilly professional facade. "Is it true, Mr. McGrath, that you own but a single Patriot Bond?"

"Yes." George's hand sought out his Patriot pin and discovered it was missing. It must have been torn off when he was taken into custody.

"Why is that, Mr. McGrath?"

"Why? Why is what?"

"Why do you have only one bond?"

"It's all I could afford. I want to buy more. I—"

The brute snorted in disgust.

"Are you a closet Constitutionalist, Mr. McGrath?"

"No, no, I'm Republicrat. I have been my whole life—a proud Republicrat."

George felt his bladder about to burst.

"Huh-huh."

"Do you believe in individual rights, Mr. McGrath? In the right to say anything you want, believe anything you want, do anything you want?"

"Uh... no, no."

"Why the hesitation?"

"It's just that, I don't know—I mean, I know we can't just say anything. It depends on—"

"Depends on what, Mr. McGrath?"

"I... I guess it depends on what you say, or what you do."

"Oh come on, enough of this," the burly fellow practically spat out. "Look at him. Green eyes, narrow chin, diamond face, wispy build, and look at the nose. As aquiline as I've ever seen."

"He fits the profile, that's for sure," said the other man.

The woman nodded, checked her pad again, and continued. "I see, Mr. McGrath, that you've never been married. Why is that?"

"No reason really. I just haven't—"

"Do you like women, Mr. McGrath?" she asked, studying him. "Are you attracted to women?"

"Of course," he stuttered.

"Do you like little children, Mr. McGrath?"

"What do you mean?"

"Just answer the question, Georgie. Don't make me beat it out you," the brute added, his casual tone belying his words.

"Why did you choose to work as a custodian at an elementary school, Mr. McGrath?"

"I don't know—I mean... it was all I could get."

"What are these for, George?" The smaller man pulled a pair of latex medical gloves out of an oversized envelope. "Do you like to play doctor, George?"

"Those are for cleaning. You know, for paint and chemicals and—what are you saying?"

How could they think such a thing of him? As hard as he worked, picking up after other people's children without complaint. Cleaning classrooms wasn't just his job. He'd always been proud to be part of a place where the republic's future was being groomed, where children were taught proper values, where they learned to put country first and respect tradition. Remembering that had always made it easier for him to overlook the grime and clutter.

He'd stood broom in hand that very afternoon, waiting for the teacher to dismiss her class, hearing her cue the children, listening as they recited in unison.

"I pledge allegiance to the flag of the United Republic of America, and to the values for which it stands: one nation under God, indivisible, with security and justice for all."

"Mr. McGrath, our BEA has provided us with probable cause to—"

"BEA? What's BEA?"

The woman frowned, annoyed at being interrupted. "Behavioral Evidence Analysis, Mr. McGrath. Our BEA, in combination with the psychogenic inventory we've conducted, has determined the likelihood you are a pedophile, Mr. McGrath—a pervert who preys upon innocent children." For the first time her professional facade withered, and George saw the wrath she'd held in check. "I have children of my own, Mr. McGrath, and I plan to make certain they're safe from you and all the degenerates like you."

"No, no, you're wrong. I would never... I couldn't. What evidence could you—?"

At that, the brute lunged at him and they both hit the floor. George's kidneys were pressed painfully against the chair's metal supports, his cuffed hands crushed beneath their combined weight as the enraged interrogator strove to choke the life out of him.

Just as suddenly, the brute was pulled off him and maneuvered out of the room by the smaller man, leaving George lying there, soaked in his own urine, gasping for breath.

He closed his eyes to avoid the glare of the lights and tried to think, but denial clouded his mind. This wasn't happening. He hadn't done anything. All he'd done was turn on his television, settle into his overstuffed chair, and take off his shoes.

He remembered wondering what the president would talk about in his address to the nation. Would he detail the glorious victory over Finland, or maybe announce an improving economy? Perhaps he'd unveil the new five-year plan George had heard about. It didn't matter. Whatever the president said, George knew he would be reassured. Things would be better. The republic was in good hands.

On the screen he'd seen the commander-in-chief pass through a gauntlet of New Glories, looking healthy, sharp, fearless. The assemblage of dignitaries, generals, and journalists stood as one, and George did likewise. When the president assumed his position behind the podium, everyone, George included, sat back down.

"*My fellow Americans, tonight I come to you with an important message. That message is... the nation is strong.*" Applause erupted, and the president waited for it to subside before continuing. "*We are strong, not only at home, but around the globe, where American military might is feared by the enemies of democracy. We are strong because we are one nation under God, undivided in our purpose—our resoluteness to crush the malevolent minions of iniquity.*"

Again he waited through the applause, punctuating it with a booming declaration. *"Nevertheless, the war against insidious terrorism and autocracy is far from over. It's a battle in which we must remain ever-vigilant, like the colonial farmer, musket in hand, watching for redcoats crossing the Potomac. Like the Army tank commander, waiting for the Nazi panzers to come rolling over the hills toward Bastogne. Like the Marine sentry gazing eagled-eyed over the ruins of Fallujah, on guard against the next wave of marauding Islamic fundamentalists.*

"Eternal vigilance is the price of security. Yes, my fellow Americans, we are strong, we are vigilant, and we understand the rules have changed. The world has changed, and we must change with it. There are limits to freedom, limits necessitated by the war in which we find ourselves—a war of ideologies. To counter foreign influence and domestic insurgency, we've had to suspend certain rights for the good of the nation... for the good of us all.

"Good Americans need to be watchful against all possible threats. Look around you. Do you see something suspicious? Do you know what that person over there is doing? Did you hear something that didn't sound right? If you're not sure, if you have doubts, report it.

"Be alert. Be observant. Bear witness."

The familiar credo echoed through George's head even as the president recited it.

"Remember too, good Americans need to be careful what they say. This is no time for dissent. Dissent is a sign of weakness. This is no time for weakness. This is a time for—"

"Help Mr. McGrath back onto his chair," said the woman in charge as she and the man in the tan jacket came back into the room. The big fellow wasn't with them.

"It looks like George has pissed himself," he said, pulling George up from the floor.

"Did you wet the bed as a child, Mr. McGrath?" asked the woman.

"No... no. I never—"

"Is that what your mother's going to tell us when we ask her, Mr. McGrath? Or is she going to tell us an entirely different story?"

His mother? What did she have to do with this? Was it a coincidence his mother had called him just the other day, for the first time in months?

"We're going to release you, Mr. McGrath—for now."

"You mean I can go?"

"Yes. But we'll be watching you, George."

He wanted to tell them if they'd been watching him they'd know he's innocent... but he didn't. All he cared about was getting out of there—getting home. He just wanted to put it all behind him. A mistake had been made. That was it. It was over.

oOo

He felt better once he got back to his normal routine the next morning. However, immediately after arriving at work, he was called to the superintendent's office. No one spoke to him as he passed through the building. The only acknowledgment of his presence were looks of repugnance and an exchange of whispers.

"Sit down, McGrath," the superintendent said, glancing over the tops of the papers he was perusing.

George sat and waited through an extended silence.

The superintendent placed the papers on his desk and signed the top sheet.

"We're letting you go, McGrath."

"Letting me go?"

"Yes, your services are no longer required by the school district."

"I... I don't understand."

The superintendent shot a look of indignation at George. "*You* don't understand. *I* don't understand how you could betray our trust in you, McGrath. I hired you in good faith. How do you think this is going to make me look? How do you think it's going to make the school district look?"

"I don't know what you mean. I... I haven't done anything."

"I think you know we can't have someone like you working in one of our schools," he said with finality. "You'll be escorted off the premises immediately. Your termination file will be forwarded to you. That's all."

George opened his mouth to protest his innocence, but the denial died in his throat. What could he say that would be believed? What words would matter? He stood, dazed and dizzy. He steadied himself and turned to the door where his escort waited.

George didn't know what he was going to do—how he was going to reverse this wrong. He headed home, thinking there must be some government agency he could appeal to. A good American, a good Republicrat, couldn't be treated this way. There must be some recourse. Did he dare bother his congressional representative? Was there a lesser official he could approach?

He was still struggling to fully accept the reality of his situation when a mobile police unit cruised by. His stomach knotted. His insides were like broken glass. The police unit disappeared around the corner, but the discomfort didn't go away.

Rapt with indecision, he found it difficult to concentrate. Everything concrete had turned to quicksand. What could he do? He was so distracted he failed to notice the surly bunch lingering near the entrance to his building.

"There he is," called out a voice accusingly.

Only then did George realize they were coming at him. He held up his hands as if the motion would hold them back.

"Wait, you don't under—"

Someone hit him and he staggered back. Several hands seized him and he struggled to get free. More blows pounded him—his head, his back, his stomach. Someone kicked at his legs, but the press around him was so constricting that many of the punches lacked intensity.

The adrenalin of desperation surged through him and he broke free, stumbling away. His attackers followed. He hurried to the nearest security cam.

"Help! Help me!" he pleaded to the camera.

Something heavy struck him from behind. As he fell he caught a glimpse of a baseball bat with an imprint of New Glory on it. More blows inundated him. The pain was overwhelming. He was crying as he passed out.

oOo

He woke to discomfort so intense he tried to slip back into unconsciousness. But he couldn't ignore his bruised body any more than he could his battered spirit. As he lay there, hurting, doubt poisoned his resolve. Could he, without realizing it... could he have done something and not known it? Could he really be a...?

No, no, he wasn't—he couldn't. It was lunacy to think so. He had to get up. He had to tell someone. Yet even if he could induce himself to stand, to disregard the pain, where would he go? Who would he tell?

George opened his eyes. It was dark, though he thought he saw a hint of daybreak stealing through a mottled pane. He didn't know where he was, but it wasn't the street. As his eyes adjusted to the faint light, he made out a ragged Patriot Bond poster hanging askew next to the window.

"He's awake."

George flinched at the sound of the voice, then located its source.

Two others were in the room with him—no, three. He could see them now. Two men and a woman.

"Where am I? Who are you?"

One of the men moved closer and squatted next to George. "Let's just say we're kindred spirits."

"Yeah," responded the woman. "Homeguard-haunting spirits."

George scooted back despite the pain, and propped himself against a wall. "Are you Constitutionalists?"

The woman laughed.

"No, George, we're not Constitutionalists."

"How do you know my name?"

"We have our sources, George," said the man squatting beside him. "We know all about you. We've read your *profile*." He said the word with loathing. "You were one of their own—a good Republicrat, weren't you?"

George nodded. "What... what do you want with me?"

"We don't want anything, George. You needed help."

"We figured, after what they did to you, you might want to join us."

"Join you?"

"Us—others like us. There are hundreds in the city alone. More across the country. We're going to set things right. No more totalitarianism and intolerance. We're going to end the tyranny and bring back government by the people—*for* the people, George."

"You're subversives."

"We're Americans," the woman countered.

"We're freedom fighters, George. We're fighting for the freedom to be different, the freedom not to be categorized because of our religion or our hair color, the freedom to disagree."

George grew dizzy. He grabbed his head with both hands. What were they talking about? Americans were already free. Security and justice for all.

"I know you've been through the wringer, George, and this is a lot to take in. So you just think about it. You're pretty banged up, so you stay here and rest. We've got somewhere to go. We'll bring you some food as soon as we can. In the meantime, you think about it. Think about what they did to you—what this government is doing to thousands of others every day with its paranoid mania and wars of aggression. Just think about it."

oOo

A short time after they'd gone, the pain subsided. It didn't hurt much, as long as he didn't move. However he felt a different kind of distress. Trying to make sense of everything that had happened caused his head to ache. He considered what the strangers had said. Maybe there was some truth to it. He could see, from his own circumstances, how things could get twisted around. Where was the justice in that?

Still, they wanted him to become a subversive, to fight against the government—*his* government. How could he? It was contrary to everything he believed. Yet, how could he go home? How could he go back to a life that had been turned so upside down? What could he do? What *should* he do?

He wasn't sure how much time had passed when he finally struggled to his feet and found the door. Dawn had chased away the dark, and he could see more clearly now. Slowly, painfully, he lurched out into the still empty street. He spotted a public safety booth and limped over to it. Once behind the dark glass of the enclosure he hesitated, trying to subdue the fragmented notions still troubling him. He punched in the civil code, banishing his wayward thoughts.

A voice responded immediately. "Homeguard. What is the nature of your call?"

George cleared his throat and said, "I need to bear witness."

Exit, Stage Right

Daniel M. Kimmel

It had been a hell of a ride, but it was coming to an end. Melania had left the White House with Barron in tow. The lying media had savaged his family but at least they had spared his youngest, not that he saw him much.

He couldn't be sure when it had all started to unravel. Was it when the Washington Post reported that Vladimir Putin was sending him messages via the delivery of his Kentucky Fried Chicken dinners? Was it when Tiffany, his daughter with Marla Maples, took a plea deal and agreed to cooperate with the investigation? Or was it when the fake news reported that his protestations about "no collusion" made about as much sense as claiming there was "no arson," because "collusion" was a charge in price-fixing cases, not in betraying the country to a foreign power?

The White House was lonely these days. Jared and Ivanka had fled to Israel under the "Law of Return," claiming citizenship which was granted by Prime Minister Netanyahu over the objections of the rabbinate. Donald Jr. and Eric were hiding out at some family property, or at least one that bore his name. His loyal staff were all gone, except for dear Kellyanne, who at that very moment was lying on CNN, claiming that her boss was the most honest man who had ever served as president, including Abraham Lincoln. And, of course, Sarah Huckabee Sanders, who was informing the press that he would soon reveal that he had received a heavenly appointment, being utterly oblivious to the fact that no one showed up to her press briefings any longer.

He couldn't understand it. He had cut loose everyone at the first sign that they had betrayed him. Priebus, Hicks, Omarosa, Bannon, Tillerson, McMaster, Spicer, Comey, Flynn, Mattis... he'd finally gotten rid of Sessions, too, who for the longest time wouldn't take a hint. After being publicly humiliated, he had insisted on continuing as Attorney-General, as if being called a "disgrace" by the president was a badge of honor.

Those sniveling cowards in Congress, like Graham and McConnell, who had continually rolled over while he was riding high, now wouldn't even take his calls. He tried reaching the Supreme Court to get pledges of personal loyalty but not even Neil Gorsuch or Brett Kavanaugh would respond, the ingrates.

With the Democrats retaking the House, it was a guarantee that he would be spending the rest of his presidency being investigated by one committee after another, over the objections of the new spineless Republican minority. That was unacceptable. He *never* paid for his actions or, indeed, for any of the bills he owed.

There was only one way he was going to get out of this that didn't end with him in prison. He reached for his smartphone—"My precious" as he called it—and began firing off a series of tweets:

Donald J. Trump *@realDonaldTrump*
Have completed my great work. Drained the swamp. Made America great again. Sent Mexico a bill for the wall. Not much left to do.

Donald J. Trump *@realDonaldTrump*
My vice president—I'll remember his name in a moment—can tie up the loose ends. Don't expect help from losers in Congress. Sad!

Donald J. Trump *@realDonaldTrump*
Tired of the witch hunt. Obama and Criminal Hillary were biggest traitors since Benedict Arnold. Deep State covered up for them.

Donald J. Trump *@realDonaldTrump*
#Fox and friends
Justice Department is a hot bed of radical leftists, though Fake News media won't tell you. Need to clean house.

Donald J. Trump *@realDonaldTrump*
Off to Winter White House for well-earned vacation and to plot next move for Trump. Expect BIG announcement soon. #Covfefe

As usual, the tweetstorm set off a frenzy on the internet. Let the lying media try to figure out what he was planning. Was he going to resign? Fire the special prosecutor? Play golf? Trump spent so much time at Mar-a-Lago that it was no longer news. What was much more surprising was when he showed up for work. That's exactly how he wanted to play it. They thought he was stupid, but he wasn't. He even told them he was really smart and a very stable genius, and they used that failed actor on "Saturday Night Live" to make him look like an idiot. Well, we'll see who gets the last laugh.

oOo

He was on the tenth hole of the golf course and he was all alone. He had ordered the Secret Service to stand down when he was on his estate. Didn't trust them. They were more likely to fire a bullet rather than take one for him, and he couldn't risk that today. The buzz was he didn't want any witnesses when he moved the ball or didn't count strokes, but he no longer cared. When the black, unmarked helicopter came in low on the horizon he tossed his club away and pulled down on his "Make America Great Again" cap to keep his hair in place, not an easy task in the backwash from the whirlybird's blades.

It alit on the green, and a man well known to Trump from his financial dealings with Russian banks stepped out.

"Mr. President, we got your message," he said. "Are you sure now is the time?"

"I'm afraid so. I knew it was over when Mueller got a hold of my tax returns after the Supreme Court refused to hear my appeal. That's why I sent out the covfefe tweet. I assume our deal is still good?"

"Of course, Mr. President. You've served us beyond our wildest expectations. President Putin extends his warmest greetings and looks forward to expressing them in person.

But now it's time to go. We need to move quickly if we're to get you out of the country."

"Lead the way."

The two men boarded the helicopter and took off into the late afternoon sun. As he adjusted his seat belt, Trump smiled. Governing had been hard. In the end, he was a real estate guy and his greatest accomplishments were still ahead of him. With his pal Vlad's help, by this time next week he'd be breaking ground on Mar-a-Lago East. And so what if Melania filed for divorce? The prenup was airtight. And Vlad's daughter Mariya was a real looker. He could see himself dating her.

After all, as a soon-to-be former president of the United States, he was a real catch.

No Excuse

Debora Godfrey

Donald J. Trump @realDonaldTrump
CROOKED HLLARY about to be jailed- for treason and colusion by ATTORNY GENERAL. Lying OVER! FAKE MEDIA says she's innosent. FAKE NEWS! FAKE NEWS!

"He's nuts. Stark, staring bonkers." Samuel Chase was clearly having a reality check moment on the first morning of his new job.

Oliver Wolcott, executive assistant to the Attorney General of the United States, smiled grimly. It had taken Chase, the bright spanking new AG, less than a day to start the five stages of wishing he had not accepted a role in the Trump White House—a new record. Maybe this guy was more on the ball than the last three? Five? Eight? However many Attorneys General there had been in the six months since Oliver was hired. Hard to remember.

"I'd read about it in the papers, but I thought it was an exaggeration. You know, liberal media and all." Chase looked a little lost, his brand new "Attorney General of the United States" coffee cup in front of him.

Oliver had just pulled the cup out of the box of six he had on a shelf, noting idly that he probably needed to get a new box; there were only two cups left.

"Nope." Chase was the third Attorney General since the beginning of the year, and it wasn't even Valentine's Day. Oliver had learned that there was no point in being subtle, and definitely no point in getting attached. He knew it was a matter of time until one or the other of them got the boot, and he was beginning to think it couldn't be too soon for himself. These days Trump seemed to be choosing the people he fired at random, so Oliver figured he might get lucky, although he wasn't sure whether being fired was bad luck or good. "That man is crazy as a loon and dumb as a post. What did he do this time?"

"Tweeted that Hillary Clinton was just about to be charged with treason and collusion by the Attorney General. That's me, and there was nothing in the briefing papers I got that even hinted about that, not to mention she couldn't be charged with treason. We aren't in a declared war."

"Welcome to our world—the land of fairy tales and midnight tweets and Crooked Hillary, the nexus of all evil. I'm surprised anyone actually bothered to get briefing papers for you." Oliver sat in the small "visitor" chair wedged between the door and the TV tray that served as a desk. Ever since the President declared that his entire Cabinet had to have their offices in the White House, space in the West Wing had been at a premium. Even though it was a former closet, at least the AG had his own office. Energy and Environmental Protection had to share. Defense, of course, had room enough for a putt-putt setup so he was ready any time the President wanted to drop by. Instead of nameplates, everyone had a small erasable board on the door (if there was a door) or their desk (if there was a desk) or on the wall (there was usually a wall), so that the names could be easily changed. By the time a requisition for an official nameplate could have been processed, the odds were that there would be a new person in the job.

"I did think it was sort of odd that the papers were addressed to Ed Rutledge. Wasn't he...?"

"God, are those still around? Must be five months or so since he was fired. I think he was the second or third AG I worked for. That was just after Trump did away with the requirement that the AG be approved by the Senate. Rutledge got fired when he refused to jail all the Democrats in Congress for disrespect. The Washington Post got hold of the story, and Trump denied he was planning to arrest them, said the whole thing was Rutledge's idea, and canned him. Normal Friday evening at the office."

"He can't act like that! He's the President! He has his finger on the nuclear button!"

The new AG had not yet moved from denial to anger.

"You do know there's no button, right?"

Chase waved his hand impatiently. "Sure, sure, everyone knows that."

"Trump didn't know it. Still doesn't, for that matter. When we told him there wasn't a button, he threw a hissy-fit, said we were trying to hide it from him. We finally had someone mock up a box with a big red button on it and a buzzer, told him it was the nuclear button. He had us put it right in the center of his desk, so that all the news cameras would be sure to see it."

"Has he hit it?"

"Yep. Twice. First time he put his Diet Coke on it by accident. The sound made him jump, spilled the Coke all over the proclamation allowing oil drilling in Yosemite. Someone made the mistake of telling him he couldn't sign the wet paper, that they'd have to make a new one. Rather than admit he'd just been clumsy, he said he didn't like the way the law was written, that he did it on purpose because it was a bad law. Exxon is pissed."

"Was that why the issue went back to Congress? He spilled his Coke?"

"Yep."

"And the second time?" It didn't sound as though Chase really wanted to know.

"Oh, that time he really was mad at Kim Jong-un, pushed the button to 'teach Little Rocket Man a lesson' so he said, because Kim called him a decrepit stuffed shirt who didn't have the self-control of an adolescent poodle. That was just before Trump told..."—Oliver put his hand on his chin, gazing at the ceiling—"McNary, I think that was it, to cancel the next elections. Called it a crisis because he had been compared to a poodle, not a real dog like a pit bull. That was what got McNary fired. He refused and by the time we found somebody willing to take the AG job, Trump had forgotten about the dog comment, and Kim was back to being his friend."

"Didn't he notice that there wasn't actually a bomb attack?"

"Nope. Miller came in with his new secretary, and by the time Trump finished staring at her... assets... he'd forgotten he'd pushed the button at all. Now, of course, he says he never did, but the box has a recorder in it, just in case."

"In case of what?"

"In case someone in this place, myself included, ever grows a spine."

As Oliver anticipated, the addition of a new Attorney General made no difference whatsoever. The AG several months before (Oliver couldn't remember who it was, but did it matter?) had closed down the official FBI Mueller investigation, but in some fashion that Oliver didn't quite understand but admired greatly, the entire mess seemed to have migrated to state court and continued slogging its way forward.

And that added to Trump's hysteria.

oOo

It was late, and Oliver was about to go home when the Attorney General called him to the postage-stamp-sized office.

"Oliver, these tweets are killing me!"

Much to Oliver's surprise, Sam Chase was still on the job two weeks later. It helped that Chase believed in not expressing any opinions if he could help it and the fact that he was the son of one of Trump's creditors. It was also his first job out of law school, and entry level positions for attorneys were hard to find. "His 3 AM tweet says 'Crooked Hillary to be arrested soon. Campaign promise filled! Just like I built the WALL to keep America safe! Best President EVER!' He didn't actually build that wall, did he?"

"No. Mexico wouldn't pay and neither would Congress. Now he keeps repeating the same thing, that the wall has been built, hoping no one will notice there's nothing there."

"And people believe it?"

"Fox News has pictures."

"I saw them, isn't that really the wall Israel put up on the West Bank?"

"Trump doesn't know that." A smile, a sad smile. "You want to tell him?"

From the slight fragrance in the air, Oliver suspected there was something other than coffee in the AG's cup. When Chase poured him some "coffee" in a second cup with the AG seal, he was sure of it. He didn't turn it down.

"I should tell him Secretary Clinton can't be charged with treason. He just doesn't listen." Despite the "coffee", Chase was tapping his fingers nervously.

"How long have you been working here? Do you honestly think he cares? Or that he's capable of that much thought?"

"Can't we get the damn cell phone away from him?" Chase was looking desperate. "The press keeps wanting interviews with me, and I can't say anything without calling him either stupid or a liar. Isn't the press secretary supposed to handle this sort of thing?"

Trump had redefined the job of press secretary, and Sean Hannity was able to combine it with his appearances on Fox, with his show now being broadcast from the former press briefing room. It worked well, at least for him; it did nothing for the distribution of truth, no doubt part of the plan.

Chase rubbed his forehead, as though getting a headache.

"What did Trump do this time?"

"When he saw that there wasn't anything about Clinton in the Daily Brief, he went off in a screaming foaming rant about her for a good fifteen minutes, two minutes longer than yesterday, and he had a troop of Girl Scouts in the Oval office at the time. There's video—you don't want to see it. It wasn't until someone brought in his Big Mac that he calmed down. Then that preacher, Falwell, came in just as he finished eating and said Clinton was the Antichrist and must be destroyed. That set him off for another hour. What's with the Antichrist thing?"

"Falwell Senior said that the Antichrist would be a Jewish male. Junior's decided that Daddy had it wrong, that Hillary Clinton is the Antichrist. He's been badgering Trump to do something to her before she brings about Armageddon."

"Jesus! Trump believes that crap?" Chase had finally moved from denial to anger.

"What Trump believes changes by the minute, depending on who he's talking to. With Falwell in the room, yeah, he believes it." Oliver shifted uncomfortably. The hard metal seat of the folding visitor's chair was really not conducive to lingering.

Chase poured each of them another drink. "I wonder if having her actually in jail would do any good."

"Yeah," Oliver said glumly. "If she were in jail..." The spark of an idea floated past. "Could we really do it?"

"Do what?" Chase asked cautiously.

Ideas born of late nights and a little too much whiskey should be thoroughly examined in the cold hard light of day. Unfortunately, Oliver omitted that step, and Chase didn't stop him.

oOo

The plan required coordination.

Oliver Wolcott drove to Chappaqua, New York, taking a number of pairs of comfortable shoes size 7, a half size smaller than the size listed on the Internet for Secretary Clinton, and a wig styled almost but not quite the way she wore her hair. Somewhat to his surprise, Hillary agreed to go along with the plan for three weeks, staying on her estate without talking to anyone outside and wearing the tight new shoes and wig until her next scheduled speaking engagement. She thought it was funny.

He and Sam worked on the format of the new report for Trump, to be delivered in the morning, just like the Presidential Daily Brief. The cover simply said, "Donald J. Trump Very Very Secret Brief"

"Just stamp 'Top Secret' all over it and he'll never know the difference." Oliver was rather proud of his handiwork.

Sam Chase would have been pacing, had there been any room within his closet.

"This will never work, you know. Trump is never going to accept that this secret brief is written in code." He picked up tomorrow's VVSB, as they decided to call their Very Very Secret Brief, from his desk. "How are we going to explain this?"

The single line of the report said "Hillary Clinton is not in jail."

"You explain it to him, say 'It's written in code, you have to think of it backwards. We wouldn't want the Washington Post to see the real information. You know how they are.' Every word exactly accurate. We really DON'T want the Post getting hold of these. Give it to him in a manila envelope with even more top secret stamps on it and stress to him that this is very very very secret, so secret you have to make sure it gets shredded before you leave his office. Hopefully, having these will help him calm down."

oOo

"Next time, you do it yourself." Chase was just back from the Oval Office. "It took forever for him to get the idea."

"What finally worked?"

"I told him that it was a secret code, a code that could only be read by someone who was a very stable genius, because everybody else would think it actually meant what it said."

"And he bought it?" Oliver hadn't really thought any of this would work, and the code part was the weakest link in the whole chain.

"Yes. I wouldn't have believed it if I hadn't been there, but he had the look of a little boy about to play a nasty joke on his big sister. And this is our president."

"What a moron."

oOo

For the first two editions, things went as planned. On Thursday, Trump chuckled when he was handed the brief, which said Clinton wasn't being moved to a new, more secure prison.

On Monday morning, he giggled like a four-year-old when he read that she was not being held in solitary, and was not asking to see a lawyer.

Each time the president was given the VVSB, Chase told Trump he couldn't tell anyone, that the information was top, top, top secret. Chase had apparently forgotten that it was a mistake to tell Trump he couldn't do anything.

Donald J. Trump *@realDonaldTrump*
CROOKED HILLARY thrown in JAIL, finelly getting what she DESERVES for EMAILS, COLUSION. MY Attorney Genral. BEST CHOICE EVER!

"Why did I go along with you?" Chase glared at his cell phone's screen, where Oliver could see the latest report from the Washington Post. "We should have known he couldn't keep his mouth shut. Now he's told everyone that she's been arrested."

"Look at the bright side. He didn't actually put your name in the tweet." Despite his upbeat words, Oliver was apprehensive. All he'd thought would happen was that Trump would stop calling for Hillary to be "locked up" for a few days, give everyone a breather from the constant harping, and, he hoped, have the whole atmosphere of the White House calm down a bit. In retrospect, that expectation was hopelessly naive.

"He probably didn't use my name since he can't remember it. He calls me Goldman half the time." Chase slipped his phone back in his pocket. "What do I tell the press? I'm getting shouted at everywhere I go."

"Just say you can't comment, there's nothing to say."

"That's certainly true."

oOo

The two men tried to cut off delivering the phony report. By the third day without it, Trump was throwing things at everyone in the room.

"I can't even enter the Oval Office anymore," Chase said desperately. "I'm afraid he'll go for my throat if I don't have the VVSB."

They made another one.

Donald J. Trump *@realDonaldTrump*
DEMS want CROOKED HILLARY out of jail. No RESPECT for LAW. She gave URANUM to ENEMY! I stopped very very BAD criminal. I WON election. BIGGEST vote EVER!

"He's just making things up now."

Chase was into the liquid courage again, and Oliver poured himself a cup. He noted that Sam seemed to be finished with the bargaining stage, and was now fully into depression. He hoped the next AG had as good taste in scotch.

"Not any more than Fox News is. The media's gone just as crazy as he is."

Fox had jumped on the non-existent bandwagon, pumping out multiple stories every day about Hillary's perceived crimes and Trump's decisive action in jailing her, talking about her cell mates, and how awful it was that she wasn't somewhere working on a chain gang. Showing hours of footage shot by the paparazzi outside Clinton's estate, Hannity declared himself horrified that the government would put an imposter in place just to fool the press into thinking that she hadn't been arrested, because everyone could see she didn't walk like Secretary Clinton, and the hair wasn't quite right.

The Wall Street Journal and the New York Times had their best investigative reporters vying with the Washington Post to determine the location of her incarceration. Rachael Maddow went through exhaustive lists proving that it really was Hillary herself on the estate, and that she hadn't actually been thrown in prison, but even Lawrence O'Donnell thought Rachael was wrong.

Jerry Falwell Jr. crowed that the Antichrist was now locked up, and good Christians should be thinking about a Final Solution to rid the world of this menace.

Hillary sent Oliver an email saying it was the most fun she'd had in years. Oliver hoped this email didn't get leaked.

"But what are we going to do? We can't keep creating this false paper forever." Chase was developing a twitch.

"Yeah, Trump's getting impatient. I can't think of anything that's going to satisfy him."

Oliver was worried. Trump had been back to throwing things that morning, and the White House staff, with the help of everyone sane left in the building, was systematically removing priceless objects for safe-keeping and storing them in the bunker under the White House, leaving inexpensive substitutes to be destroyed, trusting, rightly, that Trump would never notice.

"There isn't anything that's going to satisfy him," Chase said gloomily. "At this point, she could die and it wouldn't help."

Oliver lifted his head. Another idea glimmered.

Perhaps he should give up drinking.

oOo

Oliver created the VVSBs for the next few days.

"Hillary Clinton was not tried by a secret court."

"The only secret courts in the US are for trying spies."

"He won't care."

"Hillary Clinton was not found guilty of collusion."

Sam objected. "Collusion isn't a crime, or at least not a federal crime. Lying, fraud, soliciting money from a foreign entity to affect an election, those are crimes."

"We know that, but he doesn't, no matter how many times he's told."

"True."

"Hillary Clinton was not sentenced to life in prison."

"Harsh for something that's not actually a crime."

"Is Trump going to be happy with anything else?" Now Oliver was developing a twitch.

"I don't know. Who's he going to Tweet about if she's in prison for life?"

"I don't think that that will stop him—or even slow him down."

But Oliver was really worried. He couldn't see a logical end to this.

No more whiskey. Ever.

Donald J. Trump @realDonaldTrump
CROOKED HILLARY *conviktion proves no COLUSION by TRUMP campane. Nobody helped ME WIN. BIGGEST ELECTRIC COLLEGE WIN EVER! @realDonaldTrump*

The "conviction" worked for a week, Trump crowing about "Crooked Hillary's" defeat.

Unfortunately, someone wasn't watching him, and he tuned into channel 356 by accident instead of 360. He only saw Rachael Maddow for a moment, but it was apparently a moment too long.

Donald J. Trump @realDonaldTrump
@maddow in pay of DEMS, says CROOKED HILLARY not in jail. FAKE NEWS! FAKE NEWS! Tried, convited, sentensed. I MAKE AMERICA GREAT AGAIN!

The tantrums were back. Everyone crept around the White House, hoping to avoid the Toddler-in-Chief. The Secretaries of Labor and Agriculture signed out a conference room under an assumed name, just to have somewhere to hide. Someone "accidentally" locked Reverend Falwell in a bathroom in Melania's office to keep him away from Trump. It wasn't clear why Falwell was in her office in the first place, but, since she never went there, it was a long time before someone heard his pounding and let him out.

Oliver was running out of words to express the insanity of every day at the office, even to himself.

That still wasn't a good excuse for what Oliver did next.

oOo

Sam was getting ready to go into the Oval Office, his hand out for the latest VVSB.

"I don't think he's going to be happy with another 'Hillary Clinton isn't weeping in her cell.' He threw a stapler at me yesterday. Thank God he doesn't have better aim."

Oliver unfortunately had been collateral damage the day before, when the tape dispenser aimed at the Secretary of Education missed her and hit him. Three stitches and a big lump later, he was not feeling charitable.

He handed the manila folder to Chase.

Perhaps it would have been a good idea to warn the AG in advance what the paper said.

Oliver was all out of good ideas.

Obviously.

Chase stormed into the little alcove where Oliver had his chair (he wasn't a member of the cabinet, so there wasn't even an attempt to provide him with an office. He felt privileged to have been assigned a permanent place to sit). "My office. Now."

Because the door of the closet opened out, it was possible to close it to get privacy.

"Killed? You said she was killed by a firing squad?"

"Technically speaking, I said she wasn't killed by a firing squad."

"What were you thinking?" Sam's face was getting red. "I had to stand there and pretend I knew what emotion he wanted me to have!"

"So, out of curiosity, what did you say?" Oliver was having a hard time pretending he cared any more. He'd started his coffee earlier than usual.

"I told him that it was very sad, but she shouldn't have been a crook."

"That probably went over well. I wonder what he's going to say when she 'comes back to life' next week."

"What?" Sam had apparently not been thinking of the calendar.

"Secretary Clinton has a speaking tour starting next week to promote her new book *Why Trump Blames Me for Everything*. She'll be in New York City on Thursday."

Chase shook his head. "I don't think even Trump can figure out a way around this one. Maybe he'll lie and say this never happened."

Oliver laughed, but it wasn't a happy sound. "I wouldn't put it past him."

Donald J. Trump @realDonaldTrump
TRAITOR CROOKED HILLARY shot dead by firing squad. So sad. LUCKY SHE WASN'T PRESIDENT. SHE LOST, I WON. LANDSLIDE vote HISTORIC!

Donald J. Trump @realDonaldTrump
Failing @nytimes says CROOKED HILLARY not really dead. FAKE NEWS! Email servors prove she was a TRAITERR! I MAKE AMERICA GREAT AGAIN.

Oliver Wolcott and Sam Chase quit the White House the next day. Neither of them cared what the President threw nor who he threw it at.

The Washington Post, NY Times, and *Wall Street Journal* all gave Rachael Maddow credit for figuring out that Secretary Clinton had been at home the entire time. Lawrence O'Donnell gleefully apologized for doubting her.

Democrats were threatening to impeach the clearly insane president.

Republicans said they hadn't noticed anything unusual in the President's behavior.

At a well-attended prayer breakfast, Jerry Falwell Jr. said Revelations 13 had come to pass and they were seeing the form the Antichrist took after death.

Trump, of course, adopted the explanation that Fox News gave.

Donald J. Trump @realDonaldTrump
Jeff Bozo *@washingtonpost says CROOKED HILLARY ALIVE. FAKE NEWS! Put ZOMBIE HILLARY in jail. Being DEAD no excuse for being TRATOR. BEST PRESIDENT EVER!*

Alternative Truth III: ENDGAME

Last Interview

Melinda LaFevers

Meranda waited nervously, pen and paper clutched in hand, as the last of the security checks were completed. Interview notes only. The biggest interview of her life reduced to the modern equivalent of cave drawings. No cameras, video, no electronics.

It was odd, but what wasn't these days. No one from the media had seen the president in weeks. He had become a virtual recluse, with only incessant tweets for contact. At the thought, she instinctively reached for her phone, but it was in her purse and her purse was at the check-in station, where it had been searched, tagged, and stowed away in a locker. The insistence she give up her phone had been polite, but firm.

Finally one of the officers came over to her. These were not the suited Secret Service she expected, instead the uniforms were a dull red—muted like all the colors in this part of the White House. This was certainly not the oval office.

"Follow me, please," he said and Meranda rose from where she had been sitting and followed the man. The click-clack of her shoes echoed down the tiled and bare corridor. Despite her editor's wishes, she refused to wear high heels. She had consented to the dress, compliments of the station. It was lower cut and far more snug than she would have ever bought herself. While she missed having a voice recorder, she was somewhat glad she would be spared the embarrassment of wearing the dress on camera.

"Send me a beautiful girl," the message read. "Dressed fit to kill. I will give her my last interview."

"It is too good a chance to pass up," her boss had said. "We'll be with you."

Only they weren't. Word had been sent down that only "the girl" could come in. Meranda glanced back at the foyer, where her boss and the now useless cameraman waited. They smiled at her encouragingly. Meranda turned back around and continued to follow the guard.

When had her perceptions of him changed from "security" to "guard?" He stopped at a door and knocked. A muffled voice said something, and the door opened, revealing yet another guard. After an exchange of glances, he stepped back and motioned for Meranda to enter.

The desk was not an intricate carved wood monument, it was grey steel and the man who sat at the large desk was not the same man who had been elected three years earlier. Meranda felt a shock as she viewed the hollowed caricature before her. The frame was almost the same, but now his expensive clothes hung loose, his face lined with deep furrows, and with tinges of grey. The orange hair, yes, that was the same, but it was in wild disorder. He hunched over his phone, sending out another tweet, muttering to himself. The room smelled oddly stale and sharp at the same time.

"I'll show them. Just wait. They won't know what hit them."

When he finished, he looked up. Meranda took a step back. His eyes... his eyes held the frenzied gleam of a man whose sanity was precarious.

"You're here for the last interview?"

His eyes moved to her neckline and worked down, his smile faded into a frown as they reached her footwear. Finally, with a dismissive shake of his head, he simply gestured for her to sit.

The chair was a simple straight backed metal chair.

"Let's do this," he said.

"Yes, Mr. President. I have some questions to ask..."

"No questions," he said. "I will tell you what you need to know. You will just watch. And listen."

He leaned back in the chair, his eyes turned towards the ceiling. "I wanted to make things great. Truly great. We could have made this country the greatest empire ever." He hit his desk softly with his closed hand. "But they wouldn't listen. They wouldn't follow my orders. They left me."

It was true, Meranda knew. Two thirds of the cabinet were acting members, filling in for those who had resigned or were fired. Only Betsy DeVos and Ben Carson were left from the original.

He stood and leaned over the desk. "So here we are," he said. "Here we are." He raised his palms to the invisible masses he seemed to be addressing. He wasn't talking to her any more.

"I promised to Make America Great Again." He pointed over her head. "But they fought me, fake news. Sad. So sad."

"Enemies of the people." He shook his head. "So... we have to start all over again..."

"Start all over again? What do you mean?" she blurted the words out.

He looked down at her, as if noticing her for the first time.

"Back to the beginning," he said. "Start over. Do it right this time." The president cackled and Meranda felt fear. She looked to the guard by the door. His face was stiff.

"Take everything back to zero. To nothing. Then rebuild it the way it is supposed to be. The way I said."

He reached down and opened a drawer on the desk. "I want you to see this." He reached in the drawer and pulled out a large red button, a coiled springy cord disappeared into the drawer.

"They didn't want to make me a button." He smiled. "They wanted all the codes and checks." He stroked the button. It was a single palm sized button, it sat in a round gold frame. "I asked Vlad. He said that he had a button. Well, my button is bigger than his. Heh, heh. My button is bigger than his..."

Meranda stepped backwards to the door.

"No, please... don't..."

The man looked up at her, with a brief return to sanity.

"You know how everyone said I would fail. That I would give up?"

Meranda silently nodded.

"They were wrong."

His eyes gleamed red when the button he pushed began to pulse.

All the Prez's Men

Liam Hogan

In the last days of the once great and previously United States of America, the Prez sat before his panel of advisers. The halls and rooms of the White House were echoingly empty. So many people had let him down.

Losers.

These three were his stalwarts, his rocks. They stood by him through thick and thin and, unlike those he'd fired, had never disappointed him, never failed.

And never spoke out of turn.

Oh they had their faults, sure. Each of them had been indicted for being in bed with the Russians.

But then, who wasn't?

The Prez swept the Oval Office with gimlet eyes. Behind him the once green grass lay smoking under an ash filled sky, but still the trio waited, silent, obedient, expectant.

Eeeny, meeny, miny...

His frown deepened. Eeny meeny be damned. Was he Prez, or was he not? Executive decisions came easy to him. Really they did. Even the bigly ones. A smile crept across his doughy face as he reached to his left and pulled the unresisting adviser onto his lap.

"Hey Google," he purred in his most seductive voice, "Who should I nuke today?"

The Train

Annie Percik

The young soldier moved through the train, shifting his weight to compensate for the rocking motion. He had a private message to deliver, from the driver to the baggage master, which required traversing its whole length. His boot heels chimed on the smooth floor, announcing his approach. Uniformed crew members snapped to attention with a smart salute, passengers looked away. The official train music followed him, piped through speakers in every corridor and every compartment. He stepped in time to the rousing, military march, the notes powering his strides.

Through the opulent carriages of first class he strode, with their swinging chandeliers and velvet seat cushions. Unbroken polished wood paneling enclosed the sounds of raucous laughter and clinking glasses, party slogans and comradely back-slapping.

Further on, the carriages became more sparsely furnished, with slatted wooden seats and scratched tiling. Here, the blacked-out windows felt oppressive. Only the occasional gas lamp relieved the gloom. The young soldier picked his way between the slumbering forms of the passengers, unsure if they were really sleeping or only pretending.

The rush of air as he clambered out of one carriage and into the next revealed the speed of the train's progress. He did not dare pause to find a chink in the boards blocking the view of the outside world. As he levered open the next door, an unexpected sound reached his ears. Someone was singing. Curious, he tiptoed along the corridor and peered through the glass panel into the compartment beyond. The lack of official music drew his eye to the speakers in the top corner of the carriage. A bright blanket muffled the sound.

Below it, a man with a grizzled beard and ragged jacket balanced atop the wooden bench, clinging to the luggage rack with one hand. He swung back and forth with the motion of the train, conducting himself with his other hand, as he raised his voice in song. The young soldier watched and listened, transfixed by this entirely unfamiliar sight. Even more shocking, it was not a song he knew.

The singer's audience was made up of other passengers, similarly ragged, but gathered round in rapt attention. One or two clapped along, while the others huddled together as if seeking warmth. An elderly woman on the edge of the group glanced round nervously and caught sight of the young soldier through the glass. Her hand sprang to her mouth and she pointed silently, alerting the others to his presence and breaking him from his paralysis.

He reached for his radio. "Unauthorized activity in Carriage Fourteen."

The passengers scrambled apart and slunk back to their assigned seats.

Only the singer remained where he was, staring in open defiance, uninterested in hiding his crime. The young soldier met his gaze and shrank from the hatred he found there. The door opened behind him, bringing a blast of cold air and a troop of five masked security officers. They shoved him roughly out of the way and charged into the carriage, converging on the singer still standing on the bench. Four of them grabbed him, one for each arm and leg, while the fifth reached up to pluck the blanket free from the speaker.

Over the sound of the renewed train music, the singer appealed to his fellow passengers.

"Will no one stand with me?"

They hid their faces, turning away from the scene and curling in on themselves, studiously minding their own business.

As the guards dragged the singer from the compartment, the young soldier caught his eye again. This time, he saw desperation and a mute appeal. He stared back, maintaining eye contact until the guards opened the carriage door and carried the singer from view. The young soldier stood for a moment, looking after them. Then, with a trembling hand, he straightened his cap, turned in the opposite direction and went on his way.

Once You Start

Mike Morgan

The Chinese were shooting at them again.

Podolinsky understood their anger—he just didn't appreciate being on the receiving end of it. Functionally invisible at forty thousand feet he might be, but the methodical sweep of high-explosive shells was getting too damn close.

The air jockey wasn't alone in the aging aircraft. Jocasta Jane Mallory, or 'J.J.' as she liked to be called, was the other member of the *A Wing and a Prayer's* two-person crew. She was currently in her bunk, being thrown about by the plane's maneuvers, while he was on shift.

They'd taken to calling the flying factory *A Wing and a Prayer* because its designation was AWAP 604 and J.J. liked to invent cute phrases for letters in ID numbers. He'd pointed out AWAP didn't contain the extra 'A' that 'A Wing and a Prayer' required, but J.J. wasn't letting go of her pet name any time soon.

Her voice came through his headset. "You feel like getting above this firework display or have you decided to end everything in a blaze of glory?"

He ignored her sarcasm, keeping his hands in his lap. The aircraft didn't need a mechanic messing with the controls in a crisis; the heavily retrofitted craft flew itself.

The two operators were employed purely to step in if the autopilot failed and to make sure the onboard ovens didn't overheat during the plane's ninety-day flights.

At the first indication of trouble, the ex-bomber had shut down sulfur incineration and initiated an evasive trajectory. With the ovens off, the converted bomber's outer temperature was falling enough to be masked by its stealth capabilities. It was cooking the sulfur that gave them away.

Gaining a couple of thousand feet and veering off course half a kilometer put them outside the initial dispersal pattern. They were already up to an altitude of just over twelve kilometers, not far off the typical cruising height of a commercial jetliner, and the autopilot would continue to move them further away from the exploding ordinance.

The Chinese expected the U.S. planes to disappear as soon as they were targeted. Interceptors and missiles were useless for that reason. But if they fired off a hundred high-altitude shells, one of them might get lucky. It had happened before to other crews.

There was a part of him that wanted to snap at J.J. for not taking the attack seriously, but he couldn't work himself up to the task. It wasn't as if they were Top Gun professionals.

Despite the flying factory's military-issue hardware, the two airmen were bargain-basement private contractors. Because, as J.J. loved to repeat in her more drunken moments, if the United States government was going to drag out the end of the world, it made sense to do it on the cheap.

oOo

Podolinsky had been slow to realize J.J. was an alcoholic.

The first time he'd met her, out on the airstrip at Beale Air Force Base, she hadn't betrayed any signs of being a drunk.

The Atmospheric Remediation Program was run out of the Californian home of the Ninth Reconnaissance Wing, which was in turn part of the Twelfth Air Force's Air Combat Command. It made sense for the military to run the show; stopping planetary overheating was an issue of national security, and politicians weren't getting the job done.

The 9th RW's specialists were helping the program's civilian contractors ready the huge stratospheric aerosol factories, filling some tanks with jet fuel and others with sulfur. Junior Flight Officer Podolinsky was waiting for them to finish prepping his aircraft, the 604, sheltering from the blistering Marysville heat in the shadow of the craft's wide, swept-back wing. The Air Wing Commander had told him to wait for his senior officer, someone called 'J.J.'

"No way the Chinese will be able to bomb the program here," said a voice from behind him.

He turned to see a woman in flight gear approaching. The J.J. he'd been told to expect, he presumed. She was in her thirties, with dark hair shaved from her neck up to an inch above her ears, the rest medium-length and gelled.

"You don't think they'd try, do you?"

She shook her head. "I think they realize how close we came to war over the island bases. They're not going to push things further by hitting targets in the continental United States. Too sane and stable for that."

Podolinsky hoped she was right.

The woman wasn't finished. "Nothing to stop them lighting up the heavens if we cross into their air space, though."

"We're not going to do that."

A grin split her features. He was trying to figure why his comment had amused her when he saw the hard copy flight plan she was holding out.

Distracted, Podolinsky barely registered that J.J. was bringing aboard multiple cases of bottled cola. The missions were long, crew were permitted to bring personal comforts.

Yeah, he was slow on the uptake. It took him four days to figure out J.J. had mixed the bottles' contents with vodka and popped on fresh metal caps.

"Listen up, Pod." She didn't notice him frowning at her mispronunciation of his name. "We've got a hella long flight ahead of us. No reason for it to be dull. How do you feel about sex?"

oOo

After evading the storm of flak, the autopilot returned the sixth-gen stealth plane to its original heading. To eke out the fuel until the next mid-air hookup with a similarly stealth-equipped tanker, the plane throttled back and resumed its fuel-saving cycling between gliding and powered flight.

For every twenty kilometers it glided, it fell one kilometer. Then it executed a powered ascent to the previous height. By only shedding a kilometer in altitude each cycle, they stayed in the sweet spot for seeding the atmosphere.

Podolinsky wondered how long it'd be before the computer switched the sulfur ovens back on. They generated a heat signature detectable by Chinese spotter drones. Too soon and they'd be done for.

His jaw muscles tightened as he imagined J.J. sneaking sips from one of her endless vodka-spiked sodas.

More than one incident over the month they'd spent in the air had taught Podolinsky to leave J.J. alone after she finished her turn at the stick. That was when she drank, progressing from boisterous to maudlin to bitter. It was the hour before her shift when she was a pleasure to be around, sobered enough by the couple of hours she'd slept to be a radiant presence.

Distantly, he heard the dull boom of another shell exploding.

The Chinese had every reason to be mad as hell.

The AWAP 604's mission was to inject sulfate aerosols into the stratosphere in the cause of solar radiation management. His first day in training, Podolinsky had asked his superior why they resumed the program, relaunching it with aircraft, so soon after what had happened out in the Pacific.

"There ain't no stopping, son," the gray-haired woman had answered. "We quit now, we get a decade's worth of global warming all at once. That'd be the end of God knows how many coastal cities. Okay, the first delivery method didn't pan out, but it worked for years. So, now we have a fleet of stealth planes to do the job. To keep this damn planet from getting any warmer."

She'd gripped his arm tight enough for him to wince. "Let me tell you, spraying the sky's like everything else that makes life worth living—once you start, there's no letting up."

The Chinese weren't letting up, that was for sure.

An eight-year-long drought caused by the aerosols was more than enough motivation for anyone to keep shooting.

oOo

"I'll show you around but pay attention. I ain't repeating any of this."

Podolinsky nodded, filled with nerves. He wanted to make a good impression, and part of him was still processing J.J.'s lewd proposition. He wondered if she'd meant it.

"What we have here is a fifteen-year-old crate. Used to be a bomber. Started off fifth-gen stealth, now it's sixth-gen. Got the usual radar-scrambling profile and fixtures. They added the new plastic skin that displays an image of the sky."

"We're invisible to the naked eye, too?"

"Don't go all wide-eyed on me, Pod. Only works at a distance. Get up close and you can see the outline clear as day."

"Still, it'll help us not get caught in other countries' airspace."

"Sure, it's great. Doesn't do squat for the heat we pump out." She gestured toward the rear of the cockpit. "Back there are the galley, the head, our cabin, the storeroom. Off to each side are the sulfur tanks. To the rear of each tank is an oven, where the sulfur is burned. We mix the resulting sulfur dioxide with oxygen and water and then spew it out the plane's ass end. Stop me if I'm getting technical."

He assured her he was following along. The vapor of aqueous sulfuric acid vented from the rear condensed onto windborne particles to create the reflecting aerosol.

"Wait, *our* cabin, you said?"

"Relax, we get bunk beds. We take turns to crash, so you'll get your privacy." She winked at him. "Kinda cramped in there. We'll have to get creative."

Looking around, Podolinsky had to agree the plane's interior wasn't spacious.

J.J. saw the face he was pulling. "AWAP 604 used to be a bomber, remember? Even with converting the bomb bay into sulfur storage, we're not left with a whole lot of room."

"Wouldn't be so bad if it weren't for so long. Why do we have to stay airborne for nearly three months?"

"And here's a man who wasn't paying attention during training." J.J. pursed her lips at him. "We need to fly slow, get the right proportions of vapor to air particles so it'll condense. Can't dump it all in one place, 'cos that'll waste most of the gas. That means we're not covering a whole lot of ground each day. But we gotta cover as much territory as possible each mission, give that aerosol we'll brew up the best chance of being blown far and wide. So, we keep going until we bake our way clean through our chemical payload. We can refuel in the air, as often as needed. Not landing saves a bunch of time."

Podolinsky grunted. "I heard we couldn't land because we'd be over countries that don't agree with the program. They're refusing assistance."

She sighed. "Yeah, there's that, too."

oOo

Two weeks in, they needed to run maintenance on the right oven. Perpetually enraptured with cute nicknames, J.J. had christened the cylindrical device the 'kitchen,' on account of how they baked sulfur with it. Podolinsky was meant to be resting, but he'd tagged along out of sheer boredom.

Grunting with effort, J.J. stretched her arm through an open access panel on the oven's side. She began scraping ash clear of the outlet pipes.

Steam given off by the high-temperature incineration of the sulfur drove turbines that recharged the plane's batteries, returning some of the power used for the sulfur ovens. That process relied on the outlets staying free of debris, so the steam could escape.

Podolinsky put out a hand to steady himself. His fingertips brushed the gray exterior of the oven. The static shock was severe enough for J.J. to see it. He failed to not shriek.

"Sweet Christ, Pod. Put your lotion on. Any more shocks like that, you'll spark a fire."

Yet again, he considered pointing out that the first syllable of his last name was "Poe" and not "Pod."

A side effect of altering the stratosphere was to dehumidify it. Dryness combined with the cold of high altitude meant plenty of static buildup. But Podolinsky hated the feel of lotion.

"If you're a good boy and bring me a cola from my stash," continued J.J., "I'll help rub in your skin cream."

"Been meaning to talk with you about those sodas."

Her expression lost all trace of jollity. "Have you?"

"Alcohol is banned on missions."

"Clever Pod worked it out."

He could feel his face flushing. It hadn't been difficult. She got garrulous after knocking back a couple. Not flat-out drunk, she was too good at hiding the effects for that, but real talkative. Once he knew what to look for, Podolinsky had noticed how J.J. was never far from one of her bottles.

"What if you foul up because...?" He gestured at the bottle.

J.J. stood, unsteady on the vibrating floor of the old bomber. "Foul up? How, exactly? Everything's automated! We're along for the ride, Pod. Don't need to be sober to scrape crud. So, lighten up."

He stared down at the floor matting.

Her voice took on a gentler tone. "Are you gonna report me, when we get back?"

Podolinsky knew she'd be fired if he said anything, her rank notwithstanding.

"Look, I only snuck three cases onboard. There aren't many left."

"Yeah?" He was grasping at the rope being thrown his way. Cruelty wasn't one of his vices.

"Yeah. Thing is, I kinda like these long hauls. They force me to clean up my act. Once the booze is gone, that's it. There's no quick trip to the liquor store for more."

He had to agree with that.

Podolinsky was faced with a decision. "Okay, J.J., I'll keep it under my hat. But we got to stick to the work schedule, right?"

"Absolutely. All systems maintained strictly according to the book. You can depend on me."

He wanted to believe it was true.

Once J.J.'s secret was out, she was less circumspect in her vodka consumption. If anything, she was getting through the 'colas' faster than before.

"You're killing yourself," said Podolinsky. J.J. was naked from the waist down, straddling him on the edge of the lower bunk.

Great as the sex was, he couldn't help but feel she was being manipulative. He didn't want to believe it, but the thought was there. Was J.J. so self-loathing and self-destructive, she was having sex with him so he wouldn't stop her drinking?

"Pod, modern society only exists so humanity can commit mass suicide without having to face up to what it's doing. Compared to that, anything I do is small potatoes. 'Sides, you ain't one to talk."

Podolinsky blinked at that.

"You drink, too," she elaborated.

"Not while I'm on duty, and I drink because I choose to."

"You choose to, eh? You ever stopped, though?"

He couldn't claim he'd tried.

"Ever got a skin-full and done something stupid 'cos of the alcohol? Ever puked in the gutter after a night out with your pals?"

There was no way he could deny that.

"And when did you start? A year ago, when you were twenty-one, or before that? 'Cos that was breaking the law."

Podolinsky had the feeling he wasn't going to win this conversation. J.J. must have a list of justifications saved up for times like these.

She murmured, "Be honest, you and me, there's not much difference."

Then she stroked parts of his body he hadn't known were sensitive, and all thoughts of trying to talk her out of drinking evaporated like clouds from a seeded sky.

oOo

"Time to hand over," said J.J., entering the galley.

Podolinsky was grabbing a late supper and J.J. was getting her breakfast. Without comment, he passed her the touchpad they used to monitor the AWAP 604's functions while away from the cockpit.

In a pinch, they could take control of the aircraft from any of the cramped compartments. There were times they had to take care of physical needs, after all, or attend to maintenance in other sections. Having someone present in the cockpit wasn't mandated twenty-four-seven.

"You look happy to be heading to your bunk," she observed.

"Beats me why the government ever started reflecting sunlight back out into space."

She slung a burrito into the microwave and hit the Start button. "You're young. You don't remember what it was like. The world needed to tackle climate change. But no one wanted to reduce carbon emissions. What choice was there?"

"Grow artificial trees to sequester carbon more thoroughly than real ones?"

J.J. snorted. "Don't hold your breath for that breakthrough."

He didn't like how she thought of him as so young. J.J. was only seventeen years older than him.

"I'm old enough to remember what color the sky's supposed to be."

She pulled the microwave open the second it beeped, gingerly hoisting out her steaming meal. "Kindergartners now are using white crayons to draw the sky. White paper, white sky, white clouds. That's what I call a waste of crayon."

"I miss the blueness. With what we've done, it looks like it's about to snow, every single day, no matter the season."

"Spectacular sunrises, though. You gotta admit that."

A thought occurred to him. "Hey, how do you know what kindergartners do?"

She walked out of the galley without another word. Podolinsky didn't understand how he'd pissed her off.

oOo

Forty-thousand feet below *A Wing and a Prayer*, there were Japanese farmers struggling to find rice varieties that could grow in the record heat. Korea would be up next, then China. Lands of suffering and desperate measures.

Belatedly, Podolinsky realized J.J.'s nickname for the plane was a play on words; stealth bombers were flying wings. He felt stupid for not getting it sooner.

His mind was drifting. It was a shift with nothing to occupy his time. All systems were working normally. Colorless gas was streaming from the rear vents as intended, trails of white on white, impossible to pick out from the ground. There weren't any hostile contacts on radar. What's more, J.J. had to be on her last box of 'sodas' by now.

His mind turned to the trail of sulfur aerosol the plane was leaving in the tropopause. The funny thing was, apart from the quantities released by volcanoes, the gas normally got into the environment as a by-product of burning fossil fuels contaminated by sulfur. The methods used by the program to tackle global warming were almost ironic.

Fleets of bombers spreading vapor. Millions of tons of gas a year. A massive undertaking.

Why had mentioning kindergartners upset J.J.? The way she'd reacted earlier, it bothered him.

He tucked the command touchpad into his flight-suit pocket and went aft to ask.

oOo

J.J. ignored Podolinsky's question, taking a nip from her adulterated cola bottle instead. Then she deflected his question with one of her own.

"You know we're only delaying the inevitable?"

OK, she didn't want to explain herself. She didn't have to. Maybe there wasn't a puzzle to solve here. Maybe it had nothing to do with why she drank. There didn't need to be a cause.

He played along. "You believe in the program, right? You see we're saving the world."

"I see we need to be doing this, but it ain't gonna work."

He must have had a face like a slapped ass, because she added testily, "Look, the program isn't curing the environment. We're puttin' a Band-Aid on the injury to the biosphere, that's all."

"We're making things better." He could hear the defensiveness in his voice.

She let out a sigh. "Yes, for now. But there are downsides to geoengineering away an environmental crisis."

Podolinsky thought of the protestors back home. The administration said the program's benefits outweighed the costs. His parents agreed with that. They were scornful of people who opposed atmospheric remediation through solar radiation management; they were proud that he'd got a job with the air fleet.

"Well, I know there are a couple of things that have changed. The sky isn't as blue..."

"What goes up comes down, Pod. Tons of sulfur-laden microscopic particles falling to ground level. People breathe it in."

"Worth it, though," he insisted.

"Wouldn't be here if I disagreed."

An awkward silence fell between them. The ceaseless rumble of the engines seemed louder than ever in the narrow space of the bunkroom.

"Something had to be done," she breathed. "Things were getting outta hand. Diseases were spreading as the climate warmed. Mosquitoes from South America came up north, bringing viruses in their bloodstreams along with 'em."

"I guess."

"Too damn young, that's your problem. You don't know. People were scared. First, there was zika. It came and went. Wasn't taken seriously. Then Oona arrived, then Rickham's Syndrome. Each new one worse than the last. Birth defects, microcephaly, babies born with chromosomal abnormalities so bad there was no way parents could care for them at home. So many of 'em."

Podolinsky remembered the passing of the Halmstead Act. Parents were paid to hand over their profoundly handicapped children to the government. No more medical bills to pay. The problem was hidden away.

Halmstead babies, they were called.

Putting the infants in special care facilities didn't fix the underlying issue. The mosquitoes still spread, still bit expectant mothers.

"We knew the risks. I got pregnant anyway. Played the odds. Didn't beat 'em." She added, "Steph is a Halmstead baby."

He felt his chest tighten.

"She's six now. Not much higher brain function. I go see her every few months. She doesn't know who I am. She doesn't understand. Shit, she doesn't understand anything. All she does is react to light. They shine a flashlight on her face, she smiles. Got a great smile."

J.J.'s voice faltered.

"I'm so sorry."

"What you got to be sorry for? Not your fault." She took a mouthful from her bottle. "Some of the other kids in the center are less severe. They can hold crayons, say a couple of words. Not Steph."

Podolinsky didn't have any words. So, he sat next to her, listening.

"Least the aerosol we spread dries things out. Sucks to be a mosquito now." Her eyes were chips of flint; gray, dead things.

"We made a world that deforms our babies before they're born. If we die out, Pod, we'll deserve it."

oOo

Podolinsky knew J.J. was right: adding huge quantities of sulfate aerosols to the tropopause dried out the air. Long story short, there was less rain on average.

The high-falutin' term was 'regional hydrologic response.' Emphasis on the 'regional.'

As the Chinese complained to everyone who'd listen, an average decline in planet-wide rainfall didn't mean that every country was affected equally. Some lost more rain than others. Some even gained rainfall.

The Chinese also observed, drily, that the places where the aerosols were being distributed correlated with where the rain was failing to fall. The program's planes didn't fly over U.S. soil.

"We fly where we fly for a reason," Podolinsky's trainer had declared during indoctrination. "We are constrained in where we can go. I'll spell it out.

"We can't go close to the equator. We'd hit the rising leg of the Brewer-Dobson circulation, which might help dispersal, but we'd also dry out South American rainforests, screw up central Africa even worse.

"We can't go further south because aerosols also deplete ozone. We need the ozone layer. Without ozone, ultraviolet radiation would send cancer rates skyrocketing. So, the aerosols must be distributed away from the weakest parts of the ozone layer, like the hole over the Antarctic. That's being sensible.

"For the good of humanity, the aerosols gotta be spread in the stratosphere *north* of the equator. If that leads to a slight drought in parts of China, well, that's too bad.

"After what they did to the Marshall Islands, I could care less."

She'd never explained why the planes didn't go farther north. Over the E.U., over Russia.

Maybe some things didn't need to be spelled out.

oOo

In the first few years of climate engineering, the United States used enormous cannons to blast canisters of sulfur aerosol into the upper atmosphere. The cannons roared endlessly, day after day, from their positions on the Marshall Islands, exemplars of audacious technology striving to buy humanity sufficient time to find a permanent solution.

The islands were a symbol of climate change. Most of the atolls had already disappeared beneath the rising waters of the Pacific. In a way, the islands were fighting against their own extinction.

As soon as the extent of the drought became clear, the Chinese navy bombed those bases into oblivion. A billion people were dying of thirst. Blasting some atolls into slag was considered restrained action in most parts of the People's Republic.

Three things emerged from that unprecedented assault on U.S. assets: somehow, both sides held back from launching nuclear missiles; the United States refused to abandon its geoengineering, transitioning to a plane-based dispersal method instead; and Podolinsky got himself a job as an air-jockey on one of those flying factories.

oOo

Forty days into the mission, Podolinsky's nightmare came true.

J.J. was drunk at the controls.

Not yet clear of Chinese airspace, the plane was under attack again. He had no clue what had led up to the strike. Most likely, a spotter drone had seen their red-hot oven signature.

The standard response to being splashed was to shut the ovens down, disappear from the drone's scopes, and change location before a high explosive barrage could cause any damage.

The plane knew how to handle it.

Staggering into the cockpit, Podolinsky saw J.J. swiping at the master touchscreen.

"What are you doing?" he shrieked. "Are you overriding the autopilot?" The thunder of detonating shells rumbled so loud Podolinsky's teeth rattled.

"Stupid thing ain't climbing fast enough."

He couldn't believe what she was saying. During evasive, the autopilot kept the plane's emissions within limits the stealth systems could handle. J.J. was pushing the engines hotter than the stealth coating could hide.

"Oh Jesus, we're visible," he said, sick to his stomach.

Shrapnel tore through the fuselage.

The U.S. had built super-cannons to launch canisters into the tropopause. Using the same technology, the Chinese had developed artillery to deliver high explosive anti-aircraft shells to the same altitude.

Dozens of alerts flashed on the flat-screen panels at the front of the cockpit. Podolinsky dragged J.J. out of her chair and stabbed the cancel symbol for manual control.

"Gonna get us killed," slurred J.J. from the floor.

He stared in horror at the screen. So many systems were failing.

The engines abruptly throttled down and the plane banked sharply. Podolinsky overbalanced, falling next to J.J.

The autopilot was back in charge, trying its best.

He met J.J.'s unfocused gaze. "We need to reach the Chinese border, abort the mission. Divert through south Asia, maybe. Find a safe landing strip closer than the U.S."

J.J. laughed loudly. "There are no friendly landing strips for us, Pod. Did you forget? Everyone hates us."

oOo

Podolinsky didn't sleep for three straight days. He fixed what he could, ditched as much weight as he could, pulled every trick he could remember an air jockey ever describing. Somehow, he kept the wounded plane flying.

Within hours of taking the hit, the software evaluated their fuel reserves, considered their position over Pakistan, and analyzed the likelihood of countries within flight range accepting a request for an emergency landing.

Podolinsky transmitted a request to his superior at Beale Air Force Base. He asked her to beg the Australians for landing permission. No one else would let a pariah plane set down. The R.A.A.F. Curlin facility looked the best bet. There was no way they could reach Cairns.

The plane didn't pause for approval—it set a heading while Podolinsky was on the encrypted channel. They'd either get permission to land there or they'd ditch off the coast. Both options were preferable to remaining in Pakistani airspace, a region not much friendlier than China.

J.J. slept until the second day following the attack. She was quiet around Podolinsky then, too shaken to help much.

Turned out she'd drunk the last of her cola during that disastrous shift.

She was out of booze.

oOo

Curlin Royal Australian Air Force base was hotter than Hades. A sergeant came out onto the airstrip to escort them from the plane to the main building where the squadron leader, the base's senior officer, was waiting for a chat.

Not knowing what was going to happen, every step from the sergeant's car to the red-brick structure was nerve-wracking. Squadron Leader Barnet was in his office. He welcomed Podolinsky and J.J. to Australia and offered them tea.

The base commander talked as they waited for the refreshments. "Safe to say, you fellows are not popular. Our press gets wind of this, there'll be placard-waving libtards lined up outside the fence within five minutes."

The tea came, and he paused while the Americans took sips.

"Going to be honest. That crate of yours is pretty banged up. Don't think you're going anywhere in it in the foreseeable. We've called your people in Cairns and they're sending a team to debrief you. Until then, I'll detail a detachment of men to guard your bird, stop anyone poking around in it. I know it has some recent stealth features your government wants kept confidential and we'll respect that. Also, reckon your bosses will want to poke around, figure out what went wrong."

That all made sense to Podolinsky. The U.S. government would be applying pressure on the Australians to leave the damaged aircraft alone.

From J.J.'s expression, she was worrying about the Air Force investigators finding three boxes worth of empty bottles and running tests on the contents.

The base commander went on, "We'll put you up in quarters here while you're waiting for your people. Small place we've got here, though. Hope you don't object to sharing."

J.J. said, "We're used to cramped quarters."

Podolinsky daydreamed about throttling her.

oOo

The Chinese agents kidnapped them from the R.A.A.F. base the first night.

Bags were slung over their heads, then they were tossed into a van. Incredibly, the Ozzies must have let it happen, because no alarm was raised.

The base commander's insistence that Podolinsky and J.J. share a room made sense now; it was easier to take both contractors if they were together.

J.J. must've shared his suspicions. He heard her snarl, "Lousy Australians, stabbing us in the back."

A Chinese voice answered. Clearly, they weren't unattended in the back of the vehicle. "The U.S. government has ignored every complaint from the Australians. Your activities are causing droughts here, too. When they face extinction, what would you have them do? Go meekly to their deaths?"

The voice grew louder and Podolinsky realized the speaker's face was very close to his own.

"Will *you* go meekly to your death, young American?"

oOo

"You have a choice," said the kidnapper's superior. "You can die for the crimes you've committed against my country. Or, you can work for us."

Podolinsky and J.J. were in a warehouse, sitting opposite a man of at least seventy. After being manhandled out of the van, their abductors had tied their hands behind the backs of the chairs, making it impossible for them to stand. The plastic bonds dug into Podolinsky's wrists.

"Work for you?" He assumed the elderly figure was a senior intelligence agent for the Chinese.

"You seem outraged at the notion. Does your company pay you so very much? We will compensate you appropriately, more than they did. Or is it patriotism spurring your loyalty? Are we not all human? Should your loyalty not lie with your species?"

Not getting any answers, the agent continued. "You will direct the sulfur aerosol into a more northerly latitude. It will then drift over the U.S.A. You'll still save the world, fight the good fight against global warming. Isn't that what you care about?"

"But, why over the continental U.S.?"

"Shouldn't the Americans share the side effects of their geoengineering equally with other nations? It would seem only fair. If saving the world is your true motivation, you can hardly object?"

Podolinsky didn't know how to answer.

The old man added, "Climate engineering is a weapon as well as a panacea. The U.S. destroys its enemies through environmental sabotage while claiming to be safeguarding the future of every nation."

"Now, you wanna play the same game." J.J. sounded furious.

"Naturally. In the haste to avoid disaster, morality was the first casualty. Why should we not adopt the Americans' own methods? We shall see if they are any better at shooting down stealth planes than we are."

"Our aircraft is damaged..." began Podolinsky.

"We built our own," replied the wizened man. "We need only experienced crew. We start with you. Tomorrow, we recruit more. Soon, we will have an air fleet also. Then, I think the Americans will want to negotiate a more equitable dispersal of the aerosol."

"We don't have a choice." J.J.'s anger was fading, replaced with bitterness.

He wasn't going to see his parents again, he realized. J.J. wouldn't see Steph again. Not unless they did the unthinkable.

"You are aware, of course, we will be monitoring you remotely. Any infraction, we ignite your fuel. You will have no opportunity for... straying from your assignments."

The agent twisted his mouth into something that was meant to be a smile. "These terms are agreeable, or should I arrange your executions?"

oOo

Podolinsky and J.J. sat in the cockpit of the Chinese stealth plane, watching the clouds pass. It was surprising how similar the new aircraft was to their previous one.

Not as puritanical as their old employers, the Chinese had consented to giving J.J. a case of baijiu, a liquor distilled from sorghum, on condition she only drank it on her down time. She'd already broken that promise.

"We only need do this for a while," she whispered, before taking a sip. "We'll buy the world time while governments figure out how to cut the carbon."

"People aren't going to stop. They don't have any reason to, not while these planes give them an excuse not to change."

"Maybe," she admitted.

"You aren't going to stop, either, are you." It wasn't a question.

"Don't plan to," she said in the exact same tone.

"You're killing yourself."

He seemed to remember saying that before.

"Sweet, stupid Pod." She squeezed his hand. Then, she let go. "We're all killing ourselves. We'd all like to stop, but we don't know how."

Podolinsky stared out the cockpit window, letting the pale sickness of the sky wash through him.

Her voice was hollow yet suffused with strength; she was drifting away but right by his side; she was gone forever and never going to leave. He would forget the shape of her face and forever keep her soul in his heart.

J.J. crinkled the corner of her mouth. "Tanks are full and there are no clouds in sight. We can fly for thousands of miles. Alone in a wilderness of desert air."

"Yes," he said.

"Hell with our overseers. Let's trash their kill switch, see how far we can go."

The U.S. government would arrest them as traitors if they went back. The Chinese would murder them once their usefulness was at an end. There was nowhere to go, and no way of stopping.

No stopping, not once you started.

Nodding, Podolinsky returned his gaze to the unceasing abyss of nothingness.

"Fuck it," he said. "Fuck it all."

Babble

Charles Walbridge

The room was dark except for the flat screen. The two men stared intently as the images began to move.

Vic: They wouldn't let us film the security guards. One joined us in the elevator for the long ride to the top floor. A second one met us when the door opened.

Once inside we took the time to film some of the opulent furnishings and decorations, really nice stuff. We won't use much of that footage. But seeing us do it should have helped put the Man in a good mood.

Eventually we were able to talk.

Vic: "Can you tell us about your retirement plans?"

Elliot : That was undiplomatic. Cut it. Open with his answer.

The Man: "I'm getting back into real estate, in a big way."

Vic: We are on a clubhouse deck. Seated in comfortable chairs, table between us. Endless golf greens beyond...

No... not really.

It's what he calls the Green Room. Quite different from the usual hospitality lounge for celebrities awaiting their turn in front of the camera.

It's a bare studio with a featureless green wall. Anything can be projected on that surface. Right now the viewer will see a sunlit golf course, with palm trees.

Elliot: I see he leans forward when he responds to questions. Communicating sincerity. Good you were tracking that.

Vic: Real estate development depends on a lot of credit, on loans. How do you regain the necessary trust? You've had a lot of bankruptcies.

The Man: "I have friends in high places, but I'm not saying who they are."

Elliot: Except for twice when he drops their names further along in the interview. Delete one of those.

Vic: *"Are those friends paying the rent here?"*

The Man: *"That's a lie. The management is paying me! I add value and prestige to the property."*

Elliot: His assets are tied up. Fines and appeals will likely eat it up in less than three years. You were wise not to bring that up.

Vic: *"I understand people are sending you money."*

The Man: *"For the re-election campaign."*

Elliot: But somehow, most of it is going into an offshore account.

Vic: *"Does your family visit often?"*

Elliot: He's stuck there because of the house arrest. Another trigger subject you avoided.

The Man: *"They come whenever they can. They have busy lives."*

Elliot: One serving time, and another one awaiting judgement. That does tend to keep them occupied. Negotiating this interview must have been a minefield for you.

Vic: *"What about your ex-wife?"*

Elliot: You should have used her name. You meant his latest ex.

The Man: *"We're on good terms..."*

Vic: *"She has custody of your youngest..."*

The Man: *"He gets here as often as he can."*

Elliot: Not according to the visitors' log... delete the following five minutes thirty three seconds where he criticizes the boy's mother. Also delete the ensuing monolog about lying media, lying opposition, lying ex-wives, and the other sex partners. Edit down to one accusation per named enemy or institution. My estimate; four minutes thirty. It will be choppy.

Vic: *"What about your friend Vladimir?"*

The Man: *"Not allowed in the country. But he's been good about that. It's illegal."*

Vic: *"How is it illegal?"*

The Man: *"Keeping him away. We could work on deals right here..."*

Elliot: The long silence that follows... keep it in. Next, it's important that he seemed to give up on the background illusion. Retain what followed; he got up and let the camera follow him past the light stands and out of the room—into the carpeted hallway. That transition shattered the golf clubhouse illusion. In the hall is a broad window with a panoramic view of the city.

The Man: *"This place has a great view. Very expensive. You pay a lot for the view."*

Elliot: The immediate foreground is a well-manicured roof garden. Lower third of picture.

The Man: *"The new fence doesn't help though. It's bulletproof glass."*

Elliot: Do a voiceover here. Explain that the garden wall has been extended upward. Thick panes mounted between supports at six foot intervals.

The Man: *"You know, the garden used to be big enough so you could land a helicopter. The fence messes that up."*

Elliot: There won't be a helicopter. The fence is not there to stop bullets. They were worried that he'd leave the premises permanently by going over the wall.

Vic: I'll keep the close where the camera closes on the Man's profile. The front-oriented daylight underlines his age.

Exterior view from street level: The camera is initially angled upward. It pulls back to show more of the building. Further and further back, still centered on the structure with its hundreds of windows. Finally, the view takes in all of it, from the narrow pinnacle to the wide base.

There is no name over the entrance.

America Once Beautiful

Gregg Chamberlain

We gasp and choke on hazy smoke
And scalding acid rain,
From strip-mined mountains slagheaps flow
Crude goo across the plain!

America! America!
We dump our trash on thee,
And cut down pines
For billboard signs
From sea to scum-soaked sea!

Guns clutched in hands, the fearful bands
Take aim at friend and foe.
With all their might, they claim their right
While school death tallies grow

America! America!
This truth is very plain.
They grin and lie
Our children die,
Our gun laws are insane!

Trade wars hold sway. We all will pay.
The future looks quite grim.
There's global pain, one per centers gain
In Cayman Island trusts.

America! America!
What message do we send?
The President
With tweets and rage
Puts children in a cage

We've sold our souls for paper gold
Gave up our freedoms dear.

With Russia now, our only friend
We'll reap what we did sow!

America! America!
Trump only loves the pomp!
He wants the wall
He promised all
He has become the swamp.

Women March

Gwyndyn T. Alexander

Lady Liberty has had enough.
She exchanged her crown
for a pink pussy hat.

She stepped down off her pedestal,
waded through the harbor
with a salute for Ellis Island,
and took to the streets,
torch in hand.

Lady Justice has been pushed too far.
She carefully put down her scales,
whistled to her guide dog,
and they marched
to the Capitol and joined the die in
with ADAPT to save healthcare
for all of us.

One by one, and two by two,
we emerge:
from our homes
from our board rooms
from our schools.

We join together,
hand in hand,
to march for our lives.

We march for our country.

We march for our children.

We march for truth.

Gwyndyn T. Alexander

Don't get in our way,
or you will be pushed aside.

We march for progress.

We march for the future.

We march for all of us,
for all of you,
even those who oppose us.

We march for healthcare,
for gun reform,
for democracy.

We march for Justice and for Liberty
and for an end to corruption.

We march for those who cannot,
for those who will not,
for those whose voices are not
being heard.

We march,
we women.

We are the Amazon warriors,
resisting tyranny and fighting
those who would silence us.

We see no beacons of hope,

and so we have become that light

so we can shine for others.

We are the candles at the vigil,

Alternative Truths III: ENDGAME

we are the source of radiance.

And we march.

We will not stop until we have won.

We resist.
We vote.
We run for office.

We march.

Skin in the Game

Harold Gross

"Are you sure, sir?" The tat-man sat, needle in hand and at the ready, but his eyes were full of concern, and not a little bit of fear.

"I am." Mark paused for a moment and then realized a bit more was needed. "No need to worry, Michele. I believe in our system, and I believe in my choices. I will do what must be done."

Mark sounded presidential even to himself. That he managed to do so without gritting his teeth from the pain that blanketed his body felt like a personal triumph. His suit was running dry as it always did this late in the day, and with it came the ever-too-familiar burn that spread slowly over his body as the lubricating layer diminished. But the diplomat in Mark knew the best policy was to put the person who was about to puncture his skin over and over again at ease.

"In that case, take a deep breath, Mr. President. Let me know if you need to stop or sneeze or, well, move in any way."

"I've been here before, Michele," Mark changed over to his more folksy approach, "so don't worry. I know the process well."

Michele still looked tense so Mark continued, "I'm sorry your first time as back-up was this unplanned, but I have no doubt you'll be just as good as Lindsey. Bet she's sorry she chose this week to be in Hawaii." Mark could see Michele relax as he rechecked the ink in his pen. Well, at least as much as anyone could when faced with the task of inking the President.

"Yes, sir. I'm sure she is." Michele, satisfied with the state of his tools, turned them on and readied himself. "Here we go, sir."

The buzz of the tattoo machine began. Michele gently braced his hand on the mask covering the President's forehead to steady his needle above the exposed nose skin, trying not to notice the President's eyes staring back at him.

His back tingled with the attention of the Secret Service focused on him. The tension building in his shoulders was immense. Man, a pre-ink bourbon sounded good right now, just to steady his nerves, but under the circumstances that had seemed like a bad idea. Instead, he rolled his shoulders and took a deep breath.

Finally, carefully, Michele lined the edges of the skin freehand with a filigree border. Next, using a stylized serif font he added the joint resolution number "S.J. 253" in the center of the untouched skin. It took all of 20 minutes to complete the work; there just wasn't that much skin. The President, though his nose ran from the buzz, never asked him for a break. Michele dabbed up the snot and covered the newly inked skin with a quick-acting salve that disinfected and sealed the area to help it heal. Finally, he stepped back, his breath coming in short gasps and sweat soaking his shirt. He held up a small mirror for the President to view his efforts.

Mark admired Michele's work and the personal statement it made. There was the number of the resolution in plain sight: a line in the sand. He could see the exhaustion in his own gaze looking back at him and the odd counterpoint of his red lips also exposed by the mask. *How did this become the face of a country?* Mark wondered. He shook off the reverie; it wasn't a self-indulgence he could afford.

Instead, he turned back to the tattoo artist. "I love it, Michele. I and your country thank you. I know it wasn't the evening you had planned, but thank you." Mark reached out his gloved hand, offering it to Michele. "Would you like a photo with me before you go? Guaranteed to be a keeper. This isn't going to happen again, is it?" His quip fell a bit flat in the room, but Michele nodded and there was a quick shuffling of individuals and a flash before Michele was ushered to one door as the President was assisted to the other.

"Mr. President?" Michele stopped and turned just before passing through the exit.

"Yes, Michele?" Mark could see Michele's face light up at the repeated use of his name.

"I want you to know that I haven't been voting to take your skin. I think you're doing a terrific job, even when things aren't working out as expected. I do believe you've been doing your best for us."

"Thanks, Michele. I do appreciate that. But I wouldn't fault you for voting either way. That is the point of it all, isn't it?"

"Yes, sir, I guess so. But it's not particularly good business for me either." Michele felt the heat of his blush at the joke, but it had all felt way too serious to him.

"That's probably true." Mark smiled, somehow making it shine despite the mask. "Thank you again for your efforts Michele. I'm hoping you won't have to make a choice between politics and business again any time soon." He turned to leave and the security detail with Michele exited through the opposite door.

"Nev." Mark leaned toward the current head of his Secret Service unit who was overseeing all the traffic in the room. "Can you radio ahead and let your people and Salvador know I'm not coming back to the residence yet? I need to get a bit more done first."

"Certainly, Mr. President. To your study then?"

Mark nodded. He knew it wasn't protocol for Nev to inform his husband, but she'd have to redeploy the guards who were there anyway. It saved a step if she did both bits of communication. As a bonus, it was easier on his face, which was feeling a bit abused after the session with Michele.

Nev fell a step behind and spoke into her wrist. "Rex is not returning to the nest. Headed to the exercise yard."

Mark smiled to himself. "Rex" was his latest codename. Rex, for the hairless cat, not the Latin honorific. He imagined the conversation amongst the group that came up with that one, and the bottles of liquor that accompanied it. When he'd heard it he let them know he didn't mind. It was a compliment, a nod to his dedication, and he didn't mind the added Latin weight, even if it was inappropriate in the good old US of A. Besides, the Agency needed to have some fun too.

The corridors were clear for his passage. Normally they'd be teeming with people, even at this hour, but there were protocols and considerations; you didn't let your President be seen in a weakened state. For a change, Mark didn't mind;

his nose was really starting to itch and he had to resist rubbing it. To distract himself, he began to run the budget numbers in his head again looking for issues.

"Sir?" Jonathan, his personal aide appeared in the procession like the invaluable and omnipresent ghost he was. "The suit team is saying it's getting late for your fluid refresh. Do you want to wait till you head back to the residence or should I send them to your study?"

Mark tried to smile, but the flesh beneath the suit was stiffening, and it was too painful. "Thank you, Jonathan, bringing them here is a good idea. But let's make it the Oval Office. I think that will work better. And then drop the reports on the Middle East situation and Midwest Infrastructure plan back at the residence. I have some ideas on how to improve them."

"No problem, sir, I'm on it. I'll have the team meet you at the Oval, and I'll see you at the residence later to be sure you have what you need." With that, Jonathan peeled off down a separate corridor as they came to one of the many junctions, already on his cell.

Mark heard Nev on her comms adjusting to the change as well. He looked back at her with an apologetic shrug. Nev shook her head and smiled fractionally to let him know it wasn't an issue, which it was, of course, but it was just all part of the Service. It wasn't like it was any skin off her nose. The phrase made Mark smile a bit too broadly and he winced.

Mark knew that Salvador was going to be mightily pissed with him for not coming straight to the residence like they'd planned, but he was fully committed now. The wording on his announcement had to be just right. Neither the Presidential Study nor the Treaty Room back at the residence had the same gravitas as the Oval.

Jack and Dan from Nev's security team opened the large door to the Oval Office and preceded him to confirm the room's safety. Even on the protected grounds of the White House, nothing was assumed. He watched the quick sweep complete, waiting for Nev's nod before he crossed the threshold.

Once in the Oval, he knew he'd made the right call. Mark could smell the room's history and it filled him with a sense of purpose and resolve. Besides, it had a better view, even in the day's waning light.

He sat down carefully behind the Resolute desk, pointedly ignoring the carved initials with which one of his predecessors had abused the wood. No amount of putty and stain had been able to fully remove the scar. Despite that one insult, its fabled history as a ship and then as a ship of State for a range of Presidents before him always provided a powerful sense of humility, responsibility, and a desire to do his best.

In fact, if it hadn't been for the perpetrator of that scar, that desire may not have changed so much. Not his desire to do well, but certainly his acceptance of the laws requiring the cost of getting it wrong. All major decisions came with a personal risk now, not just to one's reputation but to one's actual body as well. It was a good change, Mark felt. As had the four presidents before him. He might be a "hairless cat" but he was a hairless cat with a sense of pride.

As he settled at the desk, a familiar hand slipped a folder with his speech in it onto the desk blotter.

"Thank you, Ms. Milligan. You're a gem as always. Sorry about the change in venue."

With a quiet nod, his office manager slipped back out the side door.

Nev took up her post near the door opposite his desk, not having been explicitly asked to exit. Jack and Dan retreated to the opposite side of the main doors. A calm fell over the room.

Mark took a breath before opening the folder and grabbing a fat Montblanc ballpoint pen from his desk drawer. The large pen blunted the still somewhat alien-feeling gloves of his bodysuit, making them less of an impediment. As he began to edit the text, he realized he was getting better at ignoring the crude sensations and the sound of the liquid sliding around in a micro layer between the fabric and his fascia.

The momentary distraction of the realization sent his thoughts back to his first loss: HB 42. The patch on his back still mentally itched from that removal. It was when he knew he was truly committed to the office and his country.

Salvador had stood with him through that moment, holding his hand tightly, ever the proud husband. They both knew the road it presaged.

HB 42 had promised growth and jobs based on his new budget and its cuts to programs. Both his own research and the data from his advisors seemed to bear out his assumptions at the time, but within six months it was obvious it was wrong—so many people had ended up without jobs while others had simply gotten richer. The people demanded their policy changes... and their flesh. "And quite rightly so," he muttered to himself.

"Mr. President?" Nev asked.

"Sorry, Nev, that was to myself. How long till they arrive with the recharge for my suit? Starting to feel a bit dry in here."

"One second, sir, I'll find out." There was some muffled discussion followed by, "Just another few minutes, Mr. President."

"Thank you." Mark refocused on the speech, or tried to. Outside Ms. Milligan's door there were raised voices. The sound proofing muted it, but he could hear Salvador.

"Nev, let my husband in and let's get some peace in our time." He smiled, but it was a weary smile. He knew he couldn't avoid the imminent conversation, but he wished it could have waited at least until after the fluid refresh. It included a light analgesic which made the pain more tolerable, though far from absent.

Another shielded comment from Nev and the door flew open, Salvador sweeping in with two agents and Ms. Milligan actively looking the other way as the door shut behind him.

"Mark? What the hell?" Salvador's presence belied his stature. He was a small man of great energy and striking looks. Mark never tired of looking into his dark eyes or at his impeccably groomed graying mane. Twenty-five years together hadn't dulled the ache in his heart, even when he knew he was about to get a thrashing for his more recent choices.

Nev's training brought her a step closer, but Mark surreptitiously waved her away with a finger toward the door.

She nodded and stepped out to allow the couple some privacy.

Salvador was at Mark's side looking down at him and the newest tattoo on his last bit of exposed skin. His eyes were hard, and he allowed no tears to form, but neither was he able to speak. For a moment Salvador could only stare from Mark's nose and back to his eyes in rapid succession.

Mark gave him the moment and then took a breath, "I know you're upset. You have every right to be, but this was the right thing to do. And, even if it isn't when you expected it, you knew it was coming."

It was like a valve opened in Salvador's body, letting out his bubble of energy. The very life around Salvador seemed to suddenly diminish, and with it the storm that had entered with him. He took Mark's hands in his with care. "I know. I do know, but I thought we were going to talk before we risked losing this last bit of you."

Mark ignored the pain in his hands as the fabric compressed against raw flesh and nerves. Ignoring pain was part of the job at this point. "I know. And if we could have, I would. But some decisions have to be made when they have to be made. We don't know this will go against me. And, even if it does, they may not vote to exact a price. We could have years, yet, with this small bit of flesh remaining. And you're not losing me, just a touch point."

Before Salvador could respond, the doors opened again and Irfan, Lee, and Jude, the evening suit techs, swarmed over to the desk with bags of fluid, a stand, and various diagnostic devices which they started to hook up to the President's suit without waiting for permission. They were one of the few teams afforded that privilege. Nev and her team quietly retook their posts inside the doors to the room. Salvador shifted behind him, well-practiced in this dance and unwilling to move farther away.

Mark felt the cold rush of fluid as it rehydrated the gap between the outer suit and his flesh, which too quickly turned to fire on his nerves. He counted one breath, two breaths, three, and then his nerves were too exhausted to send new signals. Five breaths and the analgesics were absorbed, further deadening the pain. Mark focused on the weight of Salvador's hands resting lightly on his shoulders and put his right hand atop Salvador's left in quiet alliance and thanks.

Other than the sounds of equipment and the plastic crinkle of the fluid bags deflating, no one spoke. Once complete, the suit crew left as efficiently as they had arrived, and the Secret Service detail again withdrew behind the closed doors.

Salvador bent down and kissed the hood over Mark's head while lightly squeezing his shoulders. The refreshed fluid allowed the sensation to be more intimate and less painful than earlier, and Mark was grateful for the moment.

Salvador came around to his right, still holding his hand as he did so. "You do what you need to do. I'll be waiting for you in the residence. Just don't stay up too late." Salvador raised Mark's hand to his lips and then, letting go, took a few steps toward the door. Then he stopped, and turned. "I've never known anyone so brave or bright, *semental mio*. I knew what I was getting into when you chose this path. I'm not going anywhere, regardless of the outcome... though we may need to get a bit more creative." Salvador winked at him and turned away to walk out the way he came, knocking on the door to exit.

Mark was alone again. He looked around the room, savoring his place in it and then turned to the contents of the folder. It wasn't a big speech. It was simple and needed to remain so. He had only so much skin left to offer, after all. But he felt this was important enough, would help enough people, that it was time to try. What happened after that wasn't the point. The point was to do well and be held accountable by his country as best he could.

He swiveled around to see that the sun had fully set. The White House grounds were dark with the lights of DC beyond, but superimposed over that was his own ghostly image: a man of moderate build in what amounted to a black catsuit pumped full of liquids to protect the exposed flesh earned from the inevitable mistakes that his many years of service entailed.

He could still remember the feel of Salvador's caress on their wedding night, the touch of his lips, so long ago, before

Mark had lost any flesh. Even though it wasn't the same, they found new ways to bring each other pleasure; it was a testament to their love that Salvador had remained with him, this phantom of the man he'd been when they'd met.

In the middle of the face in the window, there was one white spot. The "tip of his iceberg" as Salvador referred to it these last many months. He could have left office or stopped seeking re-election. Probably should have. But both his husband and their girls, Alia and Mia, the greatest two bundles of joy Mark had ever hoped to know, knew he would never be happy if he wasn't serving.

This may be his last act as President, or it may not. That really wasn't the point. The point was to do the right thing. Mark smiled, realizing he had the closing to his speech to Congress and the American people. He turned back to the desk and began to write at the bottom of the page:

The point is to do the right thing. Not for me, not for you, but for everyone and to never lose sight of that commitment to one another. I ask you to hold me accountable; in fact, I demand it. Thank you for your continued trust. Thank you for the right to serve you, body and soul.

Mark put down the pen with a sigh and a smile. Now was the time for all good men to head to their homes and be with their families. The outcome would simply have to wait for tomorrow.

"Nev?" The Secret Service agent was inside almost before the sound of her name had left his lips. "I'm ready to head to the residence now."

Passing on Fire

Joyce Frohn

My Grandmother called herself a "tomboy".
She bragged that she could chop wood and bale hay as
fast as the men.
And then they sat down and read the paper while she
baked fine biscuits and pie.
She loved hunting, motorcycles and gardening.
She raised four children in a boxcar;
teaching the boys to cook and the girls to love learning.
And that dairy farm sent four children to college.
Her daughters called themselves "New Women" and
"Liberated."
They marched in protests, fought discrimination on
the job and balanced motherhood and jobs.
They aimed for medical school and seminary.
They fought for their children,
you win some, you lose some.
I call myself a feminist. College was assumed.
I love poetry, slime molds and frog cells.
I signed petitions as soon as I could write.
Some days old battles stay on and
sometimes new problems arise.
We've fought for so long.
What will my daughter call herself?
Will she be the one to say "woman"?
What battles will she fight?
Her great grandmother holds her small soft hand
in a stiff callused one and passes on the fire.

The Great White Wall

Larry Hodges

"If it weren't for those Mexican commies, we'd have flying cars by now," said General Jared, stroking his stubbled chin as he stared at the Wall in the distance. "We built that thing, and now..." Sweat dripped down his face as he balled his fists.

It was a blazing hot Tuesday afternoon, a few miles west of San Miguel, Arizona.

There was nothing in all directions but dirt, flies, and a few cacti, right up to that infuriating wall that had once belonged to them and would again someday when America was great again. He wondered how many other countries throughout history had been conquered because they hadn't thought of building a wall, but none had ever, *ever* thought of this until American ingenuity came up with the original idea. *None.*

He wore a tattered green uniform that hadn't been washed in roughly forever, with three general stars sewn on poorly with white thread on the shoulder, and an American flag and a small collection of medals pinned to his chest. On his head he wore a fading red "Make America Great Again" cap, the *Made in China* tag carefully snipped off.

"It wasn't just Mexicans," said Captain Eric. "Purty near ever'body jumped on board." He was a tall, skinny man dressed in deerskin with an old Captain's two-bar silver patch safety-pinned to a shoulder. His rail-thin frame seemed inadequate for his tall, thin backpack. Their last hope lay in that pack, it contained the General's secret weapon. "Kinda hard to make flyin' cars during an occupation." He swatted at a buzzing fly as the General tried and failed to ignore the ugly, hairy wart on Eric's chin.

Closing his eyes for a moment to get rid of the ugly sight, the General smacked Ivanka, his wooden spear, against the ground, almost impaling his worn-out boots. He'd grown up during the war, joining the insurgency when he was twelve and taking on the name of one of his heroes. He'd risen through the ranks rapidly, and now, at 26, he was a full-fledged general, an imposing figure who absolutely and positively stood 6'3" and a svelte 239 pounds, with proud memories of leading his troops to victory after victory.

"There was no occupation," he cried, looking up at Captain Eric, who was also 6'3" and two inches taller, "just a bunch of rapists and thieves we've been chasing all over the country."

"From sea to shining sea," said Eric. "Back before they took all our guns, closed our factories, and took everything we needed to fight. I guess they forgot to take the ash trees." He fondled his own wooden spear.

"But we chased them out," said the general. "A sharp stick goes into someone's gut just as easily as a steel one." He pointed his spear at the wall. "And now they cower behind the wall, fearful of our mighty forces!"

"Yes, those dirty bastards," Eric said. "And they also cower behind the Canadian wall to the north, and the Chinese, Japanese, Korean, and Australian fleets on the Pacific coast, and the British, French, and Russian fleets on the Atlantic coast, and the Latin American fleets in the Gulf. Boy, if they ever let us out of our cage the things we gonna do to them!" He smacked his fist into his hand. "*Pow!*"

"Captain, I can never tell when you're serious."

"Well, that's because…" He stopped and pointed to the east. "Look, sir, it's a dispatch!" Off near the horizon a complicated set of smoke signals were rising.

Sweat trickled down their faces to the dry ground below as they slowly and meticulously decrypted the puffy clouds.

DISPATCH FROM WASHINGTON
June 14, 2046
On this, the 100th birthday of our greatest president, we announce the end of the last stand of the Mexican losers—and the 192 lightweight countries that attacked us. Today is the day we invade their disease-ridden homeland, so sad, fake news, don't believe it, zero credibility—and

order an attack on the wall—we built it, so classy!—with our beautiful forces, as we are always winning, winning, winning, believe me! Make American Great Again! America First, Second, and Third! ATTACK! ATTACK! ATTACK!

"They really should work on them's grammar," said Eric, shaking his head. "But it's amazin' how much info you can pack into a few puffs of smoke."

"The attack is on!" cried the General. "We finally get to take down TWITTER."

"What's twitter?"

"Don't you study any history, you ugly warthog?" exclaimed the General. "TWITTER—The Wall Invented by Trump To Expel Refugees."

"Wasn't Twitter something used by... never mind." Eric looked up as more puffy signals slowly arose. "It says, *'Sponsored by FOX News'.*"

"It's time," said the General, raising Ivanka. "Muster the army!"

"The battalion, sir. An army is 100,000 or more soldiers, and we gots only 'bout a thousand. If we had twice that, we mights call areselves a brigade, wouldn't that be grand?"

"*Muster the army!*" the General screamed.

"Right away, sir!" Captain Eric grabbed his bugle and played the Assembly Call.

The General continued staring at the smoke signals. What an ingenious invention. By spreading them out every few dozen miles, they allowed coast-to-coast communications in a matter of days. Only a *real* American could have come up with such a thing.

"Give me the binoculars," he ordered. Captain Eric handed the precious device over. One of the lenses was cracked, but the General was used to that. He stared at the wall. *This time* they would defeat the Mexicans, and next to pay would be the Global Alliance.

And then, those damned Mexicans *would* pay for the wall.

As Eric mustered the army, the General snacked on fried cactus and lizard jerky. American cuisine was the best.

Soon General Jared stood before his assembled army. They mostly wore deerskin, though some still had the tattered remnants of their old uniforms. They stared across the field at the great wall. Nearly 2000 miles long and the pinnacle of American power and productivity. It was YUUUge. The Panama Canal? Winning world wars? The moon landings? By comparison, those were sad. It was the Mexican Wall that had made America great again.

"My army—" the General began.

"*Battalion*," whispered Eric.

"*My ARMY!*" roared the General, causing half the battalion to step back. "You followed me into battle in every state—"

"Technically we ain't never made it to Hawaii or Alaska," said Eric.

The General ignored him. "And chased them out of our country. Today we break through the wall and chase them to the ends of the Earth!"

His troops cheered.

"We will conquer Mexico and the rest of the world. It is our manifest destiny!"

Once again the troops cheered.

"Today we fight for honor and glory!" He raised Ivanka while the rest of his men raised their own wooden shafts.

Today they would end what had started when the United Nations, dominated by Muslims and Mexicans, condemned America for jailing those armies of crooked, criminal Mexican and Honduran and what-have-you kids who kept trying to claim asylum. In retaliation, America removed the job-killing CO2 restrictions that Obama had set loose on America in his ungodly attempt to destroy capitalism. Without these silly restrictions, America once again became an industrial powerhouse that dominated the world... or would have, if the loser UN hadn't voted 192-1 to condemn America for contributing to global climate change. So America left the UN, leaving it unable to veto the UN Security Council's declaration of a worldwide embargo on American products. Oops.

And then came the invasion. Fighting back had been long and hard, and when it was done, no tank, gun, or airplane remained intact. So they rose up with spears and rocks and chased the armored columns until they fled to their ships and behind their walls. They could run but they couldn't hide.

"Sir," whispered Eric, "you've been standing silently for two minutes holding your spear in the air. Are you reminiscing again?"

"Oh, sorry. Where was I?"

"Honor and glory. Perhaps lead them in a chant?"

"Great idea!" The General finally lowered Ivanka and pulled out his battered copy of *The Big Orange Book*, and opened it at random. "Ah, here's one!"

He raised his voice. "*Lock her up! Lock her up! Lock her up!*" The army took up the chant.

"What does that mean?" asked Eric. "Who is this woman we are locking up, and why?"

"It doesn't matter, it's catchy." It was time to act.

He raised Ivanka and raced into the field. His army followed with pounding feet, also raising their wooden spears, still chanting "Lock her up!" They had rocks in their pockets for extra ammunition. Following closely behind was the secret squad, the ones with the secret tool that was the key to scaling the wall.

The General began to tire as they approached the wall. Why had God made it so hot in recent years? He wished they could do a quick detour to the Gulf, where nonstop hurricanes at least cooled things off. But a little heat never hurt anyone. All that foolish talk of global climate change had made God angry, but America would show Him that not all humans were bad, and then he'd take away the heat and hurricanes and things would go back to normal.

But first they had to win this battle.

"Captain Eric, give the secret squad command." Eric pulled out his bugle and signaled for the troops to slow down, to allow the secret squad to move ahead.

Then Captain Eric yanked on his arm. "Sir, something's wrong," he said, as they continued to jog forward, occasionally dodging a cactus and swatting at flies.

"All is going beautifully," the General said. "We're about to bridge the wall, and there's nothing stopping us."

"That's just it," Eric said. "Where's the Mexican army? Why ain't they defendin' the wall?"

It was a good question, and for just a moment the General felt himself freezing up. Had he missed something? Had he made a mistake? It was looking too easy. Something was wrong.

No, he decided. Nothing was wrong. The Mexicans just didn't have the stomach for war as Americans did. If they were willing to give up the wall without a fight then they'd take it without a fight. And then move on, pushing the Mexicans and the rest of the Global Alliance back to the Hell that they'd come from. Someday they'd build statues to him. Maybe he'd join Washington, Jefferson, Teddy Roosevelt, and Trump on Rushmore.

"They're cowards," he finally said. "Captain, give the command for the final assault." Eric played a few more notes on the bugle. Then the General began a new chant.

"Mexico will pay for the Wall!"

"Mexico will pay for the Wall!"

"Mexico will pay for the Wall!"

The men picked up the chant. Soon they approached the base of the wall. It had once been one of the Seven Wonders of the World—all American, of course—but now it was just a worn-out gray thing, badly in need of a paint job. The General shook his head in disgust. Great job of upkeep, Mexico!

And now the secret squad brought out their secret tool, still another product of American ingenuity: ladders. It was amazing that no one else had ever thought of them. They pushed them up against the 30-foot wall. As they held them steady, American forces scrambled up the ladders.

He approached the nearest ladder and began the climb to the top, his medals jangling. Already out of breath from the long run and the heat, he found himself wheezing. But not in front of the men; he was their leader, so he sucked it up, and forced himself to breathe normally.

"Are you all right, sir?" asked Eric.

"I'm fine," he said, as he stopped for a moment to catch his breath. Damn it, he'd like to skewer whoever angered God into releasing all this heat. Finally he reached the top. He pulled himself up, trying to look dashing in his old uniform.

He looked out the other side, and there it was. The Mexican army. They were dispersed in the grassy field so as not to give an easy target for an enemy with guns. They were well-disguised as goat-herders in shepherd's outfits with wooden cane-shaped shepherd sticks, no doubt hiding weapons. Milling about were herds of grazing goats. Excluding the goats, the General estimated about one hundred of them.

His men pushed the ladders over to the other side of the wall and he and the rest of his army climbed down. It was time to go to war. Mexico would pay.

The General raised Ivanka. "*Attack!*" The American army charged with their spears and rocks. The Mexicans kept hidden whatever weapons they had and only defended with their shepherd's sticks while the bleating goats fled. The Mexicans quickly surrendered, several of them rubbing their heads from hard-thrown rocks.

"We're Americans!" cried one of them in English, with a touch of a Texas/Arizona drawl.

"Why are you trying to kill us?" screamed another in a similar accent.

"They're just faking it," said the General. He ordered ten of his men to tie and gag the Mexican prisoners. "These pathetic excuses for soldiers are now our prisoners. How many times have we gone up against the enemy and defeated them?"

"Uh, none, sir," said Eric.

The General raised his voice. "Once again we have met the enemy and defeated him!" He raised Ivanka. "Nothing can stop us! *America First! America First!*"

The army raised their spears and took up the chant.

"Another glorious victory for the American army!" he cried.

"Battalion, sir," whispered Eric.

"Our army cannot be stopped! We'll sweep through Mexico and Central America, conquer South America, and then we'll go after Europe, Asia, and those other continents as they quiver in fear. They're all lightweights, believe me! So much winning! As the Spirit of Trump is our witness, we'll—
"

Captain Eric tapped him on the shoulder. "Uh, General—have you lookened into the distance?"

"Why would I do that?" asked the General as he reflexively looked into the distance. And saw it.

"There's another wall," said Eric. "A Great White Wall."

"I can see there's another wall, you warted toad!" the General snapped. "Give me the binoculars." His men had seen it too and were all staring at this glorious wall that went on forever in both directions as far as the eye could see, paralleling the Mexican Wall, but much taller. The sun reflected off its pure whiteness. Nothing could possibly be that white! But... another wall to conquer? So be it!

"Muster the army!" the General said.

"Bat—"

"*Don't say it!*" the General said, Ivanka suddenly at Eric's throat.

"Musterin' the army, sir!" cried Eric. He slowly backed away from the General's pointed stick. He quietly muttered, "Here we goes again." He raised his bugle and once again played the Assembly call. Soon, leaving behind a small garrison to guard the Mexicans, the army marched toward the second wall.

"On to the Great White Wall!" the General cried. He'd put a harpoon through the thing.

"Perhaps another chant, sir?" suggested Eric.

"Excellent idea, Captain." The General again opened *The Big Orange Book* at random and picked one out.

"Covfefe!" he cried as he raised Ivanka. His arm was getting tired from doing so. "Covfefe! Covfefe! Covfefe!" The army took up the chant.

"Where the hell didst they come up with that call?" Eric wondered aloud.

"What did you say?" asked the General.

"I said, 'Why the hell didst they build a wall?', sir."

"Good question. Probably to keep Mexicans from escaping. They all live in huts, you know, and want to come to the great USA and live off our riches. Socialists."

"Sir?" Eric said. "Look."

A small doorway had opened at the base of the white wall, like a missing tooth in the whitest set of teeth in the world. A tiny figure appeared out of it and began walking toward them.

"The enemy approaches!" cried the General. It carried some sort of rifle.

"I think it's time we brought out my secret weapon."

"The secret weapon!" cried Eric. "Comin' right up." He removed the tall, thin backpack he'd been wearing. From it he removed the secret weapon. He handed it over to the General, along with two shells.

"The enemy may have thought they stole all our guns, but some of us remember the Second Amendment," he said as he loaded the weapon. "And now I will destroy the enemy!" Putting Ivanka into a holster on his back, he held up the shotgun.

"Perhaps ten of 'em, sir," said Eric. "There's only ten shells."

"We'll start with this one."

The Mexican soldier came closer and closer. He was short, and wore what appeared to be a blue spacesuit, topped by a matching blue helmet that hid his face completely. Over his heart was the Global Alliance logo, the planet Earth under a halo, as if that made them the good guys.

He came to a stop about ten paces away. The General's eyes went wide as he recognized from pictures the weapon he was holding—some sort of assault rifle, similar to an AK-47, another of America's great inventions.

"Lay down your... sticks," said a muffled voice.

"Lay down *your* weapon," said the General.

There was a muffled giggle. "Please, General, put down your shotgun and surrender your battalion. I don't want to hurt anyone."

"I will surrender my *army* when cars fly."

"Really?" said the muffled voice. "Hold on a sec." He spoke into a wrist communicator. A moment later what appeared to be a jeep came flying over the wall. It flew halfway toward them, then came to a stop, levitating in the air. Then it landed.

"That appears to be a flying car," observed Eric. "Sir."

"I can see that, you warty walrus!" cried the General. "I was speaking rhetorically." He turned back to the Mexican. "Now surrender or else!"

"Or else what?" asked the muffled voice. "You'll shoot me with your shotgun?"

"You have ten seconds to throw down your weapon!"

"Would you like a countdown?" asked Eric. The General ignored him as he silently counted down himself.

"You give me no choice," said the General when time was up. He held up the shotgun and walked toward the Mexican enemy. The enemy kept his assault rifle pointed in the air and made no attempt to defend himself. The General pointed the shotgun at the Mexican's chest and fired.

The Mexican fell back a step, but otherwise didn't react.

Grimacing, the General raised the gun and let him have it in the head.

Again, the Mexican fell back a step, his head snapping back some. Than he stood up straight. "It's like getting hit by a small child," said the muffled voice.

"Give me more shells!" the General cried to Eric, who joined them as he rustled through the big backpack for more.

"Don't bother," said the muffled voice. Then he pulled off his helmet, dropping it to the ground and exposing a huge quantity of blonde hair and the first female face they had seen in months. Her lips were as red as the blood not flowing from her non-existent shotgun wounds, her cheeks as pale as one losing blood from a shotgun wound, which she was not, and her eyes as bright as the explosion from the barrel of a useless shotgun. She had a thin nose, dimples, and wore a necklace with a peace sign.

"A woman!" gasped Eric. "Is that the one we're supposing to lock up?"

"Idiot," said the General. "Close your mouth before you swallow a fly." He turned to the woman. "You don't look Mexican."

"Colonel Alexandra Ivanova, 133rd Battalion of the Global Alliance, and commander of the American Wall garrison," she said in a Russian accent. "I'm Russian, but the forces here are international."

The General nodded. "General Jared, commander, American First Army."

"Army? Looks like a battalion to me."

"Don't get him started!" Eric said, then winced when the General gave him a wallop on the side of the head.

"Any reason why you attacked Americans back there?"

"Those were Mexicans," said the General.

"No, they were poor, American goat herders who we allow to graze on this no-man's land between the two walls, since it's all dirt on your side. I hope it was a glorious victory for you." Then she raised a small device to her luxurious lips as a thousand men watched her every move. "Your attention, please," she said in a booming voice. The device was a loudspeaker. "Drop your weapons and you are free to go. Except for your commander, who will be taken into custody."

"My men will never surrender to a woman!" said the General. "We'll kill or capture you, and then on to that Great White Wall, which won't be so great when we're done with it."

"I don't think so," she said. "For one thing, that white wall is topped by a neutron death ray. Are you wearing lead suits? It's a pretty nice wall, and for your info, Mexico did pay their share of it—the Global Alliance shares the cost of the wall, as well as the Canadian Wall, and the navies patrolling your coasts."

"So Mexico *did* pay for the wall! *Hah!*"

She made a small adjustment on her weapon and held it up. "But you won't get to it. This AK-147 has a few extra settings."

The General leaped forward and grabbed her helmet from the ground, then leaped back. "She may have a protective suit, but I have her protective helmet! Let's see what happens to that pretty little face when it's poked with a stick and smacked with a rock! *Charge!*"

The American battalion raised their sharpened sticks and charged while Eric and the General rummaged for more shotgun shells. Ivanova smiled and held up the AK-147. A silent, thin laser beam shot out, which she pulled across the field, just over their heads, cutting off the tops of their spears. The charge came to a halt.

"Next time I aim lower," she said. She looked back at the battalion. "Now go back to your side of your wall, go back to America, go home to your families, and actually make your country great again." The American battalion very slowly began backing away, and then, one by one, they turned and ran. Soon only the General and Eric were left.

"Sir?" asked Eric.

"Get lost," the General said. Eric turned and ran.

The General turned back to Ivanova. "So... what happens now?"

She pointed at the flying jeep. "You get in the flying prison car. Then we take you to where we take all American POWs, where you'll be for a very long time—Guantanamo Bay. You'll just *love* Gitmo."

Mr. President's No Good, Lousy Day

Stephanie L. Weippert

It started with the press secretary. She issued the last-minute cancellation of the regularly scheduled briefing right after Politico released the recording. A recording from 2015 that went viral immediately because it proved without a doubt the Left's worst accusations were true. People online called it "The Smoking Gun Tape", a reference to the older technology recordings that took down Nixon. She returned to her office to print a letter everyone in the administration had in reserve for good reason. Impatient, she ripped the paper out of the printer almost too soon then grabbed her purse and stomped into the Oval Office. Anyone in her way moved with the automatic impulse humans have before a dangerous predator.

"I quit!" she screamed at him. "I have had enough of repeating your LIES—"

She never got to the end of her sentence because a Secret Service agent appeared at each arm. Her mouth snapped shut. She pulled her elbows from the agents and straightened her jacket, a contemptuous gray-suited bird. She continued in a more normal tone, still flanked by the agents. "As I was saying," the anger in her voice gave it a hiss, "I have had enough of repeating your lies, Mr. President. I am tired of being made a fool of by common reporters. I am done going out there and taking it for you." She took an envelope out of her purse and slapped it hard on the pristine blotter between them. "Goodbye." She turned to face the agents and added, "And I will escort myself off the premises." Head held high and with two agents in tow, she walked out feeling really fucking good for the first time in months.

"Don't need ya' anyway, Ya'cow!" Mr. President yelled as she left. He spun in his chair like a bored child, his cellphone between his hands. He mumbled to the phone in his hands, "Definitely a 1, am I right? Yeah, I'm right."

One of the three young men assigned to accompany Mr. President at all times, officially as aides, but more like babysitters, answered as he got up and walked over. "Yes, sir, a one. You got it right there. Now, it is almost time for your meeting with the Vice President, sir. Please give me the phone. Y'know how he hates when you ignore him." The Aide reached for the smartphone.

Mr. President batted his hand away. "He's not here yet. You can't have it until he gets here."

The aide pulled his arm back with a heavy sigh.

The minutes passed. Mr. President occasionally chuckled to himself over something on Twitter. The three Aides returned to sitting on the Oval Office furniture, their own smartphones in hand.

The Vice President entered and the Aides leapt to their feet. He waved away their respectful greetings and sat himself in the comfortable chair with a true politician's smile. "How are you doing today, Mr. President?" He had found that using the title in his greeting helped make conversations with him run smoother.

The Aides exited. Neither man seemed to notice.

"Great." Mr. President's gaze never left the phone in his hands. "Never better." His lazy spin brought the back of his chair to face the vice president.

The Vice President let his true feelings show until the chair spun back around.

"I'm here about—" The Vice President's sentence got drowned out by a commotion outside the door. A woman's voice yelled loud enough to carry into the room. "I don't care who the fuck he's with. I need to see the president! Now!"

The door burst open and Mr. President's Secretary of Homeland Security stomped in. Her face blushed red, but it wasn't from embarrassment. This woman had fire in her eyes. She stopped and the agents surrounding her moved just enough so she could be seen by both men at the desk.

After a moment to catch her breath, she said, "Mr. President, I have supported you for a very long time, but after what Politico released today..." Her expression turned horrified and her words stopped. She took a deep breath as she shook her head. "I can no longer support your crack-pot policies. More importantly, I will not." She took a step forward, which made the agents stiffen, but she only tossed a single piece of paper on his desk. "I resign, immediately." She straightened her jacket, took a deep calming breath then turned and left.

Mr. President stopped his spin and placed his spray-tanned hands on the desk. "What was that all about?" he demanded, but before the Vice President could answer, they were interrupted once more.

Another cabinet secretary had arrived. This time the acting Attorney General. Congress hadn't even had time to confirm this one yet. He nodded to the Vice President in the chair as he approached the desk. In a tone of great contempt, he said, "Sir, I can no longer be a part in the atrocities." He held up a white envelope and set it next to the Press Secretary's letter. His expression flashed with surprise at the name on the paper, but he quickly calmed his expression. "My resignation," then turned around and left.

The President looked at his Vice President with confusion and shock; rendered for a short moment in his long life speechless. Before either man regained their composure, another cabinet position entered and tendered a resignation, followed by another. Mr. President cursed and threatened them, but it didn't stop people from resigning, at first in groups of two and three, then larger groups, and finally a messenger carrying a bundle full of envelopes with resignations, including ones tucked inside for every single one of his Aides.

"Losers! Every living one of them. How could they be that stupid? SAD!" Mr. President raged at his Vice President. "Not to be a part of this administration? I have the best administration! Better than any President ever! I have thousands of people begging to work here!"

"Indeed you do, Mr. President," the Vice President answered him as a grandfather would answer his two year old grandchild. "And I'm sure you will vet them and hire them tomorrow, but tonight, I want to thank you for your service. All our goals were achieved, thanks to you, sir." He pulled another envelope from his pocket and held it between his hands, then looked at it. "We couldn't have done it without you, but we did it. Every deregulation, every tax cut, all the affronts to God made illegal, everything we wanted, absolutely everything." He paused as if he couldn't quite believe it. "And now that we got want we wanted..." He looked up and smiled. "We don't need you anymore." He stood to drop the envelope on top of the pile already on the desk then added, "And since the Russians don't really care regarding the details on how this country falls, they agreed to our withdrawal from the arrangement." He let the envelope drop. "Goodbye, Mr. President. My next appointment is with the special prosecutor's office. Rest assured sir, your name will never be forgotten."

The President swore at his Vice President's retreating back, but stopped once the doorway cleared. A small Latina woman stood there, the Senate Sergeant of Arms. Two burly men flanked her, each with an FBI badge and sidearm. She paused to open the double doors wide, and as the armed FBI agents surrounded him, he heard her voice clearly. "Mr. President, you are under arrest."

The first thing they did was confiscate his cellphone.

The Nature of the Problem

Thomas A. Easton

Samuel Atwood, "Discovery of a Novel Microorganism in the Human Brain," *PLOSOne*, **June 3, 2020.**

Abstract: Bacteria such as *Wolbachia* and parasites such as *Toxoplasma* are known to reside in animal brains and affect their behavior. Such bacteria are rare in humans but do exist. A bacterium related to *Wolbachia* has been observed in a small number of human frontal lobes. It appears to suppress activity in nerve cells involved in rating the credibility of information. A suitable treatment may lead to a reduction in willingness to believe unsupported claims.

Press Release, September 5, 2020
National Institute of Allergy and Infectious Diseases (NIAID)

We wish to announce an intensive vaccine development effort targeted against *Wolbachia credulensis*, a recently discovered human brain parasite. *W. credulensis* appears to make people vulnerable to erroneous beliefs. While found throughout the nation, *W. credulensis* appears to be much more common in certain regions. A successful vaccine will remove an immense hazard to public well-being.

Press Release, September 6, 2020
Church of the Holy Revelation

This morning, the Reverend Michael P. Augerson told the audience of his front-running cable show that yesterday's announcement by the National Institutes of Health of an attack on the so-called "gullibility germ" is actually an attack on organized religion.

"University of Maryland researcher Samuel Atwood is the Anti-Christ," he said. "A fraud! There is no such thing as a gullibility germ! And if there were it would have nothing to do with religion!"

InfoWhores.com, posted September 6, 2020, 8:23 PM

Libtard professor Samuel Atwood thinks he's found a gullibility germ! If so, he's more infected than anyone else! But he's not alone! Somehow he has convinced the National Institutes of Health to pay him mucho bucks to develop a vaccine that will cure people of this so-called germ.

It's all part of the conspiracy against True Conservatives, folks! They're going to tell you it's just another vaccine. And they'll mix it with the flu vaccine so everyone gets it! But it will really be a mind-control drug! Just like the ones in the chemtrails you breathe every day!

Infowhores.com, posted September 6, 2020, 8:32 PM

Vaccines are evil! They cause autism! It's been proven! Protect your kids—Say NO!! to doctors!

InfoWhores.com, posted September 6, 2020, 9:17 PM

Samuel Atwood
213 Washington Blvd, Linthicum Hts, MD 21090
(410) 722-0299
atwoods@umb.edu

Nice-looking house, huh? Guy must make a ton of money making up that gullibility germ stuff.

And no, that cross-hair over his front door doesn't mean a thing. The software just put it there and I can't do a thing to get rid of it. ;)

Laboratory Break-In, Burglars Arrested

Baltimore Sun, September 8, 2020

At 2:30 AM this morning, University of Maryland security guards responded to an alarm and found intruders in the lab of neurobiologist Samuel Atwood. One security guard and two intruders were injured in a brief exchange of gunfire. One intruder escaped.

University Professor Accused of Fraud
Baltimore Sun, September 8, 2020

Samuel Atwood, a Professor of Neurobiology at the University of Maryland, has been accused of fraud. Members of White America, a Conservative activist group, admitted that they broke into his lab and stole computer files. Those files prove, they said, that his claim to have discovered a gullibility germ is fake. "He made it up," they said. "He's a member of the Progressive Democrats, and he just wants to destroy the modern Conservative movement."

Professor Atwood claims his lab computer contained no files related to the study in question. "They made them up," he said. "And I'm no Progressive Democrat. I'm a Democratic Pragmatist, solid for evidence-based policy."

Professor Atwood is on administrative leave while the University investigates the fraud charges. He is not permitted to enter his office or lab, and he may not teach his courses.

Swastikas Painted on University Professor's House
Baltimore Sun, September 13, 2020

When University of Maryland Professor Samuel Atwood woke up this morning, he found the front of his house painted with swastikas and threats such as "Ur kids ar ded Bigget!"

Professor Atwood commented: "One more darned thing! You would not believe the hate mail I've been getting. I turned it all over to the FBI but they say they can't do a thing. Hate isn't a crime these days."

Senate Announces Hearings on NIH Gullibility Vaccine Effort
Washington Post, October 1, 2020

Senator Lindsey Graham (R-SC) has announced that the Senate Committee on Appropriations will hold hearings on whether and to what extent the National Institutes of Health may have overstepped its responsibilities by announcing an attack on gullibility. "We do not need research into basic human behavior or fake public health threats," he said. "Especially when it threatens the national economy."

He was apparently referring to claims by White America radio host Jack Pingree that reducing the gullibility of American citizens would irretrievably damage the advertising industry and the retail economy.

Senator Graham also noted that one topic of the hearings will be whether the nation truly needs scientific research agencies such as the National Institutes of Health and the National Science Foundation. "It may be time to deauthorize these agencies and use the money for additional subsidies for the coal industry and tax breaks for American businesses. Besides, what has scientific 'research' ever done for us besides promulgate myths such as evolution and global warming?"

Professor's Children Missing
Washington Post, October 17, 2020

Professor Samuel Atwood's two daughters were allegedly kidnapped as they waited in line for the school bus yesterday afternoon. Reportedly, a black SUV pulled up in front of the school and two men jumped out, grabbed Delia Atwood, age 7, and Jasmine Atwood, age 9, and threw them into the SUV. The car had no plates. Police say there has been no ransom demand so far.

Dr. Atwood is the discoverer of the controversial "gullibility germ." Standing red-eyed beside his lovely wife Cathryn, he said, "It is obvious what they want. They want me to undiscover it, or say it was all fakery. But I can't do that. It's real." His wife nodded.

NIH Issues Request for Proposals for Studies of *Wolbachia credulensis*
Washington Post, October 20, 2020

NIH spokesperson Cecily Panet explained that it is very difficult to treat brain infections. "There is a barrier between the blood and the brain that keeps most medications out of the brain. But *Wolbachia credulensis* is a living organism. It has to infect a victim in childhood and migrate through the body to the brain. While it is doing so, it is vulnerable. A vaccine could prime the body's immune system to destroy it. And sometimes vaccines work even inside the brain."

"But we really need to learn a great deal more about the organism's life cycle before we can find a solution. This is why we are asking for research proposals. We are hoping researchers will quickly gain insights into the nature of this organism and into ways of preventing or curing infection."

InfoWhores.com, posted October 22, 2020, 5:02 AM

Fraudulent researcher Samuel Atwood is still under investigation for his "gullibility germ" fakery. And now the National Institutes of Health wants to fund more research so they can stop people believing in God and American Exceptionalism.

These Atheists HAVE to be stopped! Even if that means a Second-Amendment solution!

[link to September 6 post giving Atwood's address and contact information]

Atwood Children Killed, White America Operatives Arrested
Washington Post, October 25, 2020

The FBI successfully tracked the kidnappers of Delia Atwood, age 7, and Jasmine Atwood, age 9, daughters of Professor Samuel Atwood, discoverer of the gullibility germ. Unfortunately, by the time they were able to obtain a warrant and break into the White America hideout, the girls had been shot.

Alleged Atwood Killers Free on Bail
Washington Post, October 27, 2020

An anonymous person posted $10,000,000 bail each for White America operatives Hadley Jenkins and James Richards, the alleged killers of Professor Samuel Atwood's daughters, Delia Atwood, age 7, and Jasmine Atwood, age 9. Professor Atwood is the discoverer of the gullibility germ.

Jenkins and Richards were last seen at Washington National Airport, boarding a plane for the Cayman Islands. A spokesman for White America acknowledged the two were taking a "well earned" vacation after dealing with the stress of being falsely accused of a heinous crime.

NIH Funds Six Studies of *Wolbachia credulensis*
Washington Post, November 15, 2020

The National Institutes of Health has chosen six of over 200 proposals to study *Wolbachia credulensis* in hope of finding a way to destroy or ward off this brain-infecting bacterium. NIH spokesperson Cecily Panet commented that, "We have every hope of rapid progress. If a vaccine seems possible, however, it will still take years to develop the vaccine and gain approval for its use in humans. It would be much better to find another way to interrupt its life cycle. Fortunately, one researcher—she prefers not to be named at present—has preliminary evidence that *W. credulensis* is also found in dogs. If people catch it from their canine companions, that offers interesting possibilities."

FacePlant Post, November 16, 2020

Alan Firkin: Can we make people less gullible by vaccinating dogs against the gullibility germ? It looks like maybe, since dogs seem to get the bug too. But are dogs gullible? Well, if you've ever pretended to throw a ball and laughed as silly Rover ran off thinking he was chasing it, the answer to that question is a real no-brainer.

Atsani Dasch, "Survey of *Wolbachia credulensis* Incidence in Domestic and Wild Canids," *PLOSOne*, submitted January 5, 2021.

Abstract: Almost all domestic canids tested had colonies of *Wolbachia credulensis* in frontal lobe tissue. Colonies were absent in only pugs and wild canids (wolves, coyotes, jackals, and dingos) tested. *W. credulensis* spores were detected in domestic canid blood and saliva. Salivary contamination in particular provides a plausible route for human infection.

Samuel Atwood Obituary
***Washington Post*, January 12, 2021**

Professor Samuel Atwood, discoverer of the gullibility germ, committed suicide on January 10. He left no note.

His daughters Delia, age 7, and Jasmine, age 9, predeceased him. He is survived by his wife, Cathryn, two brothers, and...

Do We Still Need NIH and NSF?
***Washington Post*, January 15, 2021**

The Senate hearing on "Do We Still Need NIH and NSF?" began today. In his introductory remarks, Senator Lamar Alexander (R-TN) said, "The National Institutes of Health and the National Science Foundation have been of immense value to this nation in the decades since they were first established. But they have gone astray by supporting research into the myth of global warming and the silliness of whether dogs are gullible. Research the nation truly needs is that supported by the Department of Defense and the Department of Energy's 'Fossil Fuel Renewal' program."

One of the first to testify was Omar Henson, retired general and a fellow of the Cato Institute. He noted that academics, especially in the biological sciences, have a very low rate of participation in organized religion. In fact, a great many are avowed atheists! They thus have nothing to say to proper members of our Christian society. "By all means," he added, "their research funding would be put to much better use as subsidies for the suffering coal industry."

Francis S. Collins, Director of the National Institutes of Health and himself a Christian, denied that all bioscientists are atheists. "The truth of science," he said, "does not depend on the beliefs of the scientists. It depends only on the nature of reality." The audience in the gallery booed in response.

Dr. Martha Jellison of Tufts University Vet School, said that if dogs are truly infected with behavior-altering bacteria, they must be cured. "It is irresponsible to let them remain ill when we have it within our power to cure them."

InfoWhores.com, posted March 23, 2021, 9:00 PM

According to the *Washington Post*, the National Institute of Health reported today that it has proven relatively simple to prepare a vaccine against canine *Wolbachia credulensis*. Initial tests will begin immediately.

The vaccine consists of killed *W. credulensis* cells. Similar vaccines are effective against a wide variety of diseases in cats, dogs, and people. If successful, it should be possible to administer the vaccine as part of the standard rabies vaccine.

Since no one worries about autism in dogs, this does not seem to threaten us humans. However, we do know this bacterium can affect animal behavior. How will removing it affect the way our dogs act?

Early Tests of Dog Vaccine Very Promising
Washington Post, June 14, 2021

The National Institute of Health reports that the anti-*Wolbachia credulensis* vaccine for dogs has so far proved both safe and effective. The best news is that in adult dogs it seems to kill even bacteria in the brain.

According to NIH spokesperson Cecily Panet, NIH is already discussing license terms for the vaccine with Novartis, maker of the routine rabies vaccine.

Dogs Aren't Much Fun Anymore
New York Times, September 4, 2021

The anti-*Wolbachia credulensis* vaccine for dogs is brand new, but it has already been administered to 17 million pets. The good news is that it kills the gullibility germ. The bad news is that dogs don't play fetch anymore. You throw the ball, and they just look at you, as if to say, "Oh, c'mon!"

Animal shelters are reporting a rise in cat adoptions.

Sanctuary for Those on Simmer

Sarah Bigham

We are the tired from so many
heartbreaks and handguns and
AR-15s we are the poor of
esteem, dignity, and basic
respect we are the
not-so-much-huddled-as-brazen
masses marching to be free of
hate mongers and pubic
grabbers in a land we say is
for everyone, if you've got
privilege let us live let us love
let us teach let us pause let us
work let us scream let us in let
us out let us choose let us
breathe let us stay let us heal
let us rest let us sing let us
rise we will rise we will rise
we will rise we will surely
rise oh, shall we rise!

Gold and Ivory

Cobalt Jade

Wren and Maisie chose the porch swing to have their tea party. They spread Maisie's doll quilt on the sun-warmed cushions, arranging around it two small guests: Maisie's sad-faced teddy bear with movable joints and Wren's Barbie doll.

"Wow. She's really old." Maisie tried to bend its dirty plastic legs, but they remained stiff and splayed from the hip. "Let's give her some tea."

Maisie's mother had left them a plastic pitcher of lemonade which they filled the toys' tiny cups with. They drank themselves, swirling the ice like grown-ups, watching the robot combine work its way across the field.

"How old is she?" The doll's cheerful smile, still visible, was at odds with its battered condition.

"I think a hundred," Wren said, with the vague sense of time of a five-year-old. She helped herself to a "tea sandwich"—a cracker with butter spread on top and a thin slice of cucumber—and munched. "My great aunt gave her to me. She had her when she was a little girl."

Wren's family of bioengineers had moved to Murdoch last year from Minneapolis, and Maisie still felt slightly inferior to her. Because she felt the urge to match Wren's claim, she said, "My family has old stuff too."

"What kind of stuff?"

Maisie glanced across the shimmering wheat where her mother directed the hired men to clear a patch of brush. "I can show you." She marked her mother's distance from the farmhouse and where her attention was focused, then gestured to her friend. "It's inside. Shhh. Grandma's at the computer. She won't like it if she sees us snooping."

Wren nodded and closed her mouth dramatically, holding her finger over her lips. Maisie slowly opened the screen door to avoid the squeak and they tiptoed down the hall. Grandma's back was bent as she peered over the computer screen, remotely guiding the combine. Classical music played, hiding the creak of the floorboards from her. Like two field mice, the girls skittered past the office and up the stairs, heading for the patch of sunlight that came from the doorway to Grandma's room.

Once inside, Maisie knew where it was. Or as she thought of it now, as "It." It was only shown to the family on the Fourth of July. There was a ceremony about It, filled with both wonder and ghoulishness. It was always presented at dusk, before the firecrackers came out, when Grandma told the story of how, long ago, It had been made and where she had found It. After that telling they all gave thanks, by which Maisie understood the threat of It had been neutralized and the destruction it had caused would never happen again.

Maisie had asked to see It at times other than the Fourth of July, but Grandma always brushed her off. Maisie felt insulted that she thought she would lose It or harm It. She wasn't a baby anymore, and Grandma should know that.

They crept over to the bureau. Maisie knew It was kept in the lower drawer, the same place her and her brother's birth certificates were kept along with other important papers. After the last holiday she had glimpsed Grandma sliding the drawer shut when the day's festivities were over, the last of the s'mores consumed.

The girls knelt on the rug before the drawer. "Ready?" Maisie whispered. Wren nodded.

Maisie opened the drawer and rooted around. In the back, behind the balled-up woolen socks worn only in winter, her hand grasped the box. She pulled it out.

The box was wrapped in a short-napped velvet cloth, which made Maisie think of grown-up things like bottles of bourbon and fancy dresses worn at parties. She unwrapped it in the August heat as the ceiling fan steadily clacked. The box was made of cardboard and had once held jewelry. She took off the lid and displayed the interior to Wren in her small, soft hands.

Wren's anticipation turned to disappointment. "That's it?"

The object nestled on the cotton looked like a squashed, dirty pancake, something that their toys might eat on the little tin plates that matched their cups. "It's a tooth," Maisie said.

"Oh!" Wren took in the bit of yellowish human enamel embedded in the disk, as well as a flash of gold from an object similarly battered and flattened. Both were embedded in a mass of dirty asphalt and gravel.

"It's from the war," Maisie explained. "After the old capitol was destroyed and the people took over. Don't touch it," she warned.

Wren jerked her hand back. "Why?"

Maisie couldn't explain, it was only what her family had always said. She thought it was because they feared whatever evil was left in the relic might jump out and infect her. "It's the old man's tooth, the dictator's. When he tried to escape, they stopped him on the road. The tanks and trucks drove over him, all day, all night, until there was nothing left of him. Only this." It was the story Grandma had told her, and she kept the same cadences. "Grandma picked it out of the road when it was all done."

"Yuck!" Wren's small face scrunched up into a grimace. "Was he alive when they did it?"

"I don't know." Maisie achieved some satisfaction in having affected her friend so much. The gruesomeness of the relic fascinated her. She was at the age where functions of the body had become interesting to her; she was always asking how food was digested and hearts beat, and what happened when they stopped beating. Her parents always said the tooth was a thing of the past, the old country that didn't exist anymore, and should be saved so the same thing wouldn't happen again.

"What's the gold in it from?"

"A button maybe?"

Wren eyed it like a suspicious crow with her head tilted to the side. "My mother helps the farmers clone their dairy cows. Do you think someone could clone the old man with that?"

Maisie scratched her scalp under her ponytail. "Why would anyone want to? He was evil. He hated women... and girls," she amended, including Wren and herself. "He did horrible things."

"But what if someone did? And he would be a... a... boy, walking around, causing trouble, getting the other boys to cause trouble. That's why the war happened, right?"

The thought had never occurred to Maisie before. She felt a chill. Maybe that was why Grandma kept it hidden.

"I think we should bury it," Wren said.

"My grandma would see it's missing. I'll get in trouble."

"I have modeling clay. We can make a fake one."

"No." Maisie felt a danger prickling her stomach. She had always thought of the relic as a distant piece of history that didn't concern her. Now, it did, and she didn't want any part of it.

"We can burn it. The next time there's a barbecue."

She remembered Grandma's voice: *We swore we would never suffer that way again.* If they destroyed the relic, would those words still hold weight? No one talked about the old man, or any old men, really, any more. If this last piece of him was gone, would all the bad things he had done disappear as well? And what about the good things, like the lives she and Wren had now?

Life seemed fragile all of a sudden. An illusion.

A noise from downstairs spooked her. Maisie quickly wrapped the box in the velvet and pushed it back into the drawer.

"Girls?" Grandma's voice called. "What are you doing up there?"

"Wren had to use bathroom, Grandma." Maisie motioned to her friend. "Come on."

At the bottom of the stairs they saw that Grandma had her apron on. "I talked to your mom, Wren, and she said it would be okay for you to spend the night. Would you like to? We have fresh corn for dinner."

"Oh yes!" Wren said, hopping with excitement.

"You can stay in Maisie's brother's room if you want. He's been sent away for his Conditioning. Why don't you take in that picnic tray from the porch and help me shuck this corn."

They went back on to the porch where Mama was coming in with the men, their shock collars forcing them to walk in a straight line as the van pulled up to take them back to the labor dispensary. Maisie waved at her, and Mama waved back, smiling. Soon Aunt Hailey would be home from the Grange meeting with Jessa and her daughter, and they would all sit down together for dinner, demonstrating what was right in the world.

Contributors

Sara Codair, the cover designer, is also a writer. They live with a cat, Goose, who "edits" their work by deleting entire pages. They teach and tutor at a community college, write when they should be sleeping, and read every speculative novel they can get their hands on. Sara's debut novel, *Power Surge*, was published by NineStar Press in October 2018. Find Sara online at https:saracodair.com/ or @shatteredsmooth.

Nathan Ockerman programs software, raises cats, sees to the care and feeding of a spouse and daughter and is the chief cook and clothes washer of his abode. He also has a beard.

Jim Wright is a retired US Navy Chief Warrant Officer and freelance writer. He lives in Florida where he watches American politics in a perpetual state of amused disgust. He's been called the Tool of Satan, but he prefers the title: Satan's Designated Driver. He is the mind behind Stonekettle Station (www.stonekettle.com). You can email him at jim@stonekettle.com. You can follow him on Twitter @stonekettle or you can join the boisterous bunch he hosts on Facebook at Facebook/Stonekettle. Remember to bring brownies and mind the white cat, he bites. Hard.

Gwyndyn T. Alexander is a feminist, activist poet. She lives in New Orleans with her husband Jonathan. They are owned by Scout, who is a cat. She is a dick, but they love her.

When not writing, Gwyndyn creates fabulous feathered barrettes and headpieces. Her motto is "Be the parade you want to see in the world!" She is the author of Digging Up My Bones, also available from B Cubed Press.

David Gerrold was a runner up for this year's one-line biography award, coming in only six votes behind Vonda N. McIntyre's one-line bio.

K.G. Anderson is a late-blooming speculative fiction author who writes fiction as if it were fact. (Maybe, somewhere, it is.) She lives in Seattle with the love of her life and his 50,000 rare and not-so-rare books, writing branded content by day and fiction by night and weekend. Visit http://writerway.com/fiction/ for a list of her publications and links to the stories you can read or listen to online.

Sarah Bigham writes from Maryland where she lives with her kind chemist wife, three independent cats, an unwieldy herb garden, several chronic pain conditions, and near-constant outrage at the general state of the world, tempered with love for those doing their best to make a difference. A Pushcart and Best of the Net nominee, Sarah's poetry, fiction, and nonfiction have appeared in a variety of great places for readers, writers, and listeners. Find her at www.sgbigham.com.

Gregg Chamberlain is a not-so-average Canadian (he can't skate and doesn't care about the NHL even though he can name the teams and thinks the greatest player of all was Number 99) but he does enjoy puns so be warned. He lives and writes in rural Ontario with his missus, Anne, and their trio of cats, who let the humans think they are in charge. He is proud, yes, PROUD, to be part of the Alternative Universe, and when not thinking up new ways to give a certain Cheesehead a good jab where it counts, occupies his time with speculative fiction ranging from fun to serious. You can find his stories, if you dare, with *Daily Science Fiction, Apex, Ares, Mythic, Nothing Sacred, Weirdbook*, and a variety of other magazines, e-zines, and original anthologies. "America, Once Beautiful" owes its origins to Gregg's fond memories of Mad Magazine song parodies, and he still thinks that "America the Beautiful" should be the American national anthem.

Natalie Zellat Dyen, a former French teacher and technical writer, is now a freelance person. She lives and writes in Huntingdon Valley, PA. Her fiction and poetry have been published in *Philadelphia Stories*, *The MacGuffin*, *Damselfly Press*, *Willow Review*, *Every Day Fiction*, the *Schuylkill Valley Journal*, *Wordhaus*, and the *Jewish Writing Project*. Her non-fiction has appeared in *Global Woman Magazine*, the *Montgomery County Times Chronicle*, and the *Philadelphia Inquirer*.

For more information about Natalie, visit her website: www.nataliewrites.com. And look for her short story collection, *Finding Her Voice*, which is coming out in the summer of 2019.

Thomas A. Easton is a member of the Science Fiction and Fantasy Writers of America, a well-known science fiction critic (he wrote the SF magazine *Analog's* book review column for 30 years), and a retired college professor. He holds a doctorate in theoretical biology from the University of Chicago. He writes textbooks for McGraw-Hill on Science, Technology, & Society and Environmental Science. He started publishing science fiction in the 1970s, and since then he has published about fifty science fiction and fantasy short stories, ten SF novels, and several anthologies, of which the latest, coedited with Judith K. Dial, is *Fantasy for the Throne* (Fantastic Books, 2018).

Joyce Frohn is married with a teen-aged daughter. She has begun a career as a writer after graduating from college with a biology degree. And she understands that this doesn't make sense. She has been published in a variety of places from *ClarkesWorld* to receipts and political postcards. She is also a church librarian. She has two cats, a lizard, chickens and a Patreon account.

Debora Godfrey has been published in *More Alternative Truths: Stories from the Resistance and Alternative Theologies*. She lives in a modern commune on Bainbridge Island, Washington, with one husband (part time), a dog, a bird, and a variable number of lawyers.

Bruce Golden's short stories have been published more than a hundred times across a score of countries and 30 anthologies. *Asimov's Science Fiction* described his novel *Evergreen*, "If you can imagine Ursula Le Guin channeling H. Rider Haggard, you'll have the barest conception of this stirring book, which centers around a mysterious artifact and the people in its thrall." His latest book, *Monster Town*, is a satirical send-up of old hard-boiled detective stories featuring movie monsters of the black & white era. It's currently in development for a TV series. Learn more at his website.

Most often writing as **Harold Gross**, Harold is also published collaboratively as Gordon Gross. He's previously appeared in *Fantasy & Science Fiction*, *Analog*, and *Pseudopod* as well as several anthologies and sites in the US, UK, and Australia. Most recently, he placed several micro-tales in Story Seed Vault. In addition to writing, Harold has also been caught in live and recorded performances on stage and screen and regularly publishes spoiler-free movie reviews on haroldgross.com and @haroldgross, with 2000 reviews and growing.

Yorkshireman **Philip Brian Hall** is a graduate of Oxford University. A former diplomat and teacher, at one time or another he's stood for parliament, sung solos in amateur operettas, rowed at Henley Royal Regatta, completed a 40 mile cross-country walk in under 12 hours and ridden in over one hundred steeplechase horse races. He lives on a very small farm in Scotland. Philip's had short stories published in the UK and Canada as well as the USA. His novel, "The Prophets of Baal" is available as an e-book and in paperback. He blogs at sliabhmannan.blogspot.co.uk/.

Paula Hammond is a professional writer, based in London, but forever dreaming of a castle with its own writing turret in the wilds of Wales.

To-date she has written over 50 fiction and non-fiction books. When not frantically scribbling, she can be found indulging her passions for film, theatre, sci-fi, and real ale.

Larry Hodges is an active member of SFWA with 101 short story sales and four novels, including "When Parallel Lines Meet," which he co-wrote with Mike Resnick and Lezli Robyn, and "Campaign 2100: Game of Scorpions," which covers the election for President of Earth in the year 2100. He's a graduate of the six-week 2006 Odyssey Writers Workshop, the 2007 Orson Scott Card Literary Boot Camp, the two-week 2008 Taos Toolbox Writers Workshop, and also has a bachelor's in math and a master's in journalism. In the world of non-fiction, he has 13 books and over 1800 published articles in over 160 different publications. He's also a professional table tennis coach, and claims to be the best science fiction writer in USA Table Tennis, and the best table tennis player in Science Fiction Writers of America! Visit him at larryhodges.com.

Liam Hogan is an Oxford Physics graduate and award winning London based writer. His short story "Ana", appears in *Best of British Science Fiction 2016* (NewCon Press) and his twisted fantasy collection, "Happy Ending Not Guaranteed", is published by Arachne Press. Find out more at his website, or tweet @LiamJHogan

Cobalt Jade is a GenX writer who lives in Seattle, Washington and has written science fiction and fantasy for many years, with a love for erotica and horror.

Daniel M. Kimmel is the 2018 recipient of the Skylark Award, presented by the New England Science Fiction Association. He was a finalist for both the Hugo Award for *Jar Jar Binks Must Die... and other observations about science fiction movies* and the Compton Crook Award for best first novel for *Shh! It's a Secret: a novel about Aliens, Hollywood, and the Bartender's Guide.* His specialty is humorous SF, citing Robert Sheckley as a major influence. He's had short stories in several anthologies including

Alternative Truths. Trained as a lawyer, he briefly practiced before shifting to a career as a film critic, which he has been doing since 1983. His other novels include *Time on My Hands: My Misadventures in Time Travel* and his latest, *Father of the Bride of Frankenstein.* You can learn more at his website.

Melinda LaFevers is an arts educator with a wide variety of interests and hobbies. She is a teacher trainer with the Arkansas A+ program of arts integration. As a historical interpreter, she brings children and teachers into the world of castles or log cabins, providing hands-on experiences to bring history alive. Hobbies included spinning and handweaving. She learned storytelling at her mother's knee, and includes stories, music, and traditional and original songs and music in her programs. Her published writings include one non-fiction book, a magazine column on traditional herbal use, and a number of short speculative fiction stories. One of her goals is to get a story published in almost every genre possible. So far she has done alternative history, paranormal, horror, steampunk, fantasy, and political fiction. She is currently working on a poetry chapbook, several short stories and hopefully someday, she will have that fantasy novel finished. She occasionally blogs at Melinda's Obscure Thoughts. To read more of her work, check out her Amazon author page.

David Brody Lipton studied creative writing and education at Sarah Lawrence College and Boston University. His stories have been published at *CommuterLit* and *Aftermath* Magazine. He lives with his family in Houston, TX.

Louise Marley is an award-winning writer of fantasy, science fiction, and historical fiction. Twice the winner of the Endeavour Award, her work has been shortlisted for the Campbell Award, the Tiptree Award, and long-listed for the Nebula Award. Much of her work is influenced by her first career as a classical singer, most recently her novel *Mozart's Blood.* As Louisa Morgan, she is the author of *A Secret History of Witches* and *The Witch's Kind.* Louise lives on the

Olympic Peninsula in the Pacific Northwest. You can learn more about Louise and her books (and her Border Terrier) at www.louisemarley.com.

Mike Morgan wrote *Once You Start* after his best friend died of organ failure resulting from alcoholism. His friend tried to stop drinking, many times. But sometimes, when you start doing something, it turns out you can't stop, no matter how hard you try and no matter how much support you get from the people who love you. And that is a terrible and true thing. Mike also worries about global climate change. He thinks we're all addicted to living the way we live. We're heading toward catastrophe and we need to make some hard choices—we need to stop what we're doing. But we're not likely to stop what we're doing if we won't even admit what we're doing is wrong. When Mike stared down at his friend's grave he thought this: people who won't face up to reality are doomed to self-destruction. And sometimes it's easier to die than to live. These are also terrible and true things. But they don't change other, equally important, truths: we should keep trying to stop, to change, to make the hard choices. Because it is better to live than to die, and there is no way of destroying yourself without harming others. One day soon, we will discover together whether we have succeeded or failed in stopping our collective self-destruction. Mike hopes we succeed. Either way, he misses his friend. He understands why things turned out the way they did. He still wishes things had turned out differently.

Kurt Newton's fiction and poetry have appeared in numerous places, including More Alternative Truths. He works in the field of health physics and is exposed to radiation on a daily basis. He considers his job far less dangerous than the current administration.

Annie Percik lives in London with her husband, Dave, where she is revising her first novel, whilst working as a University Complaints Officer. She writes a blog about writing and posts short fiction on her website. She also publishes a photo-story blog, recording the adventures of her teddy bear. He is much more popular online than she is.

Frédéric J.A.M. Poirier has many scientific publications that nobody reads. He also authored a lot of computer code that is still regularly read—by computers. Occasionally, he writes for humans' consumption too. He likes to say that he is a doctor, but deep down he knows his PhD is useless. He has a secret wish of being brutally murdered repeatedly in stories written by his long-time friend and author Bruno Lombardi.

Robert Walton is a retired middle school teacher and a lifelong rock climber with many ascents in the Sierras and Pinnacles National Park. His publishing credits include works of science fiction, fantasy and poetry. Walton's historical novel Dawn Drums won the 2014 New Mexico Book Awards Tony Hillerman Prize for best fiction and first place in the 2014 Arizona Authors competition. He co-authored "The Man Who Murdered Mozart" with Barry Malzberg, which was subsequently published in F & SF in 2011. Most recently, his story "Do you feel lucky, Punk?" received a prize in the 2018 Bartleby Snopes dialog only contest. Please visit his website for more information about him.

C. T. Walbridge is retired from working as an environmental biologist. Currently tracking the co-evolution of human and artificial intelligence. Stories include "High Cotton," in Intel's *Tomorrow Project* Anthology (2011); "The Lost Gospel Writers," in *Alternative Theologies* (2018); and "Babble" in *Endgames* (2019). He follows the algae news the way some people follow the sports news. He's apparently incapable of writing dystopian fiction. Even hideous hordes of invading aliens are good guys. Or... they're doing the best they can.

Stephanie L. Weippert

My writing began with a slug. Let me explain.

Several years ago, a local sci-fi convention sent out a call for short stories for an anthology, and since their mascot was a slug, every story had to have a slug, either as an important character, or an important plot element. The idea tickled my funny bone, so I wrote my first story to send out for approval. It wasn't accepted of course, but the writing bug bit and with the help of my tolerant, wonderful husband, I've been writing ever since. After eight years of hard work learning the writing craft, my first book, *Sweet Secrets*, was published by TANSTAAFLPress.

Thanks Jess, Ben and Sara

it's been a hoot.

Bob B

58986596R00126

Made in the USA
Columbia, SC
29 May 2019